TRAPPED

BOOK 1

THE VIRTUAL GUARDIANS

KATRINA KAHLER & RICHARD AXTELL

Table of Contents

1. Main Menu

YOU

ARE

DESTROYED

It was the fifth time Jason Finn had been destroyed today. It was beginning to annoy him. The bright red words flashed on the television as Jason, defeated, lay back on his bed and stared at the ceiling of his bedroom. What was *wrong* with him?

KNIGHTS OF ZEMBALOR was Jason's favorite game. He was really good at it. He had always been really good at it. Really, really good. In fact, he might even have gone as far as saying that he was one of the best.

Playing under the username *Finn2Winn*, Jason had trained his knight up to level one hundred in record time. He had all the best gear, all the best weapons. He even had the secret 'super rare' achievement where you defeat the final boss in under five minutes in just your underwear! Hours of his life had been spent playing this game. Weeks. Years!

So, yeah, Jason was pretty awesome at *KNIGHTS OF ZEMBALOR*. There was no doubt about it.

But today, it felt like he was playing the game for the first time. Another player, *SparkleKitten24,* had set about making his life as hard as possible. She stabbed his knight when he wasn't looking. She completed quests before he had a chance to. She angered a dragon and then *left him all alone* to be roasted and chewed up like a knight-shaped burrito.

Worst of all, the player kept saying things like:
Loser!
Haven't you played this game before?
and
Wow, that was embarrassingly bad.

Jason was losing points; he was being taunted, all by *SparkleKitten24*.

He sat up, staring at the screen through narrowed eyes. Jason was going to get the points back and prove *SparkleKitten24* wrong. Even if it took him *all night*. Jason was ready. He picked up the controller and-

"Jason?"

Uh oh.

Jason was allowed to play *KNIGHTS OF ZEMBALOR*. He wasn't going to get in trouble for that. It was the pile of untouched math homework scattered all over his bedroom floor that *would* get him in trouble. He was supposed to have finished it

two hours ago.

Launching himself off the bed, Jason began frantically gathering up the pieces of paper. Maybe he could do a bit before his dad got up the stairs, and pretend he was stuck…

Too late. The door to his bedroom flew open with such force that the gaming posters on his walls shook.

Thomas Finn was an older father; he had wild white hair and wore thick black glasses. He currently looked like he had just walked through a hurricane of spaghetti and meatballs. Tomato sauce was splattered all over his face, his light mauve shirt and his white coast. The red tie around his neck matched the tomato sauce that was splattered on the rest of his clothes. He held a spatula in one hand, the way he would have held a sword. For Thomas Finn, cooking wasn't just the preparation of food; it was a battle.

"You've been playing the game again," he said, waggling the spatula. "I heard you shouting from downstairs."

"Ah, Dad." Jason scrambled back up to the end of his bed. "You know, I was just in the middle of doing my homework, and the games console just turned on all by itself! You probably heard me cry out in shock."

"Uh-huh."

"This room might be haunted," Jason added.

"And it made you cry out repeatedly, for the last two hours, and say things like 'Nooooo, how can I be defeated?' and 'Take that, filthy dragon!'?"

Jason picked an old sock out of the pile of homework and dropped it back onto the floor. "Yep. That sounds about right."

Thomas Finn took a step into the room. A piece of tomato fell off onto the carpet. "Can I see your homework? I'd like to check it."

Jason froze like a cat that has just been caught playing with the pet hamster.

"Yeeeeeeeeeeeessssss…" Jason slowly lifted the papers from his lap. His dad reached for the corner of the pile and tugged. Jason didn't let go. "Once I'm finished! I just need to check it over myself first."

Thomas raised a single eyebrow. "You said that yesterday."

"I'm… a hard worker?" Jason squeaked.

"Show me the homework, Jason."

"But what if-"

"Jason."

"I can't-"

"*JASON.*" His dad used that no-nonsense-you-are-in-a-lot-of-trouble-young-man voice. He didn't use it often. Jason knew he had to admit defeat.

YOU ARE DESTROYED.

The words fluttered in his mind again. It *really* wasn't his day. With a long sigh, Jason handed over the math worksheets.

His dad looked at them.

Jason waited.

"This is empty," Thomas said.

"I was hoping you wouldn't notice." Jason grinned, but Thomas Finn wasn't in a laughing mood.

Jason started a blabbering defense. "Math isn't *that* important, you know," he said. "In a couple of years, once you get me that camera I asked for (it's been on my birthday list for a few years now, and my Christmas list, you must have missed it), I can start my online career and I'll be making millions and millions playing games for people to watch. I'll be a celebrity. I will be set for life."

Thomas sat down on the end of the bed next to his son. He didn't say anything. Jason *hated* it when his dad went all silent and thoughtful.

"How," Thomas said after a time, "will you count your millions and millions of dollars if you can't do math?"

Jason shrugged. "I'll pay someone to count them for me."

Thomas shook his head and looked away. He may have been trying to hide a smile, but Jason wasn't sure.

"Stop trying to get out of doing the work," he

said, turning back. "You've been playing for hours. Your grades aren't going to improve at all at this rate."

"How important are grades, *really?*" Jason asked.

His dad stood up. "You need to work harder, Jason. What would Mom think?" The skin around Thomas's eyes tightened as they filled with regret at what he had said.

"I don't know," said Jason quietly. "She's not here anymore. I haven't known what she is thinking for a long time."

Jason looked down at the floor of his bedroom, kicking a stained t-shirt off a nearby chair.

"Yeah, kid, I know," Thomas said.

Jason didn't move. He just blinked away the stupid tears that were forming in his stupid eyes. He wanted to be left alone. He felt the large, warm hand of his dad ruffle his hair.

They both sat in silence for a moment.

His dad suddenly leaped to his feet. "I've got it!"

Jason looked up. "You're going to let me *never do homework again?*" he said, hopefully.

"Ha! Of course not," his dad grinned. "I'm going to *un-ground* you!"

Jason opened his mouth and then closed it again. He wasn't sure what to say.

Thomas Finn pulled his son to his feet. "Jason, you are *ungrounded*. So that means you're grounded, but instead of being sent to your room you have to *go outside*. You have to *live your life.*

Breathe fresh air. Talk to people!"

Jason's eyes widened. "What?" he said, taking a step. "Y-y-you can't do that! That's so cruel!"

But his protests were ignored. Jason watched in horror as his dad walked over to the wall and pulled out the power cable for his television. The screen went black.

"Just watch me," he winked.

Jason gasped. "You *monster*! I didn't even get to say goodbye!"

Thomas didn't reply. He just grabbed Jason by the arm and began marching him downstairs towards the front door. Jason begged all the way.

"I'll do my homework, I promise. I'll do the washing up, I'll clean the house from top to bottom, I'll even take a shower if I have to, but please please *please* don't make me go *outside!*"

His dad handed Jason his sneakers. Jason miserably put them on.

Soon he was standing by the front door to his house, coat thrown over his shoulders, shivering like a lost lamb.

"Can I go back upstairs now?" he said in a small voice. "You've made your point."

His dad opened the front door. Jason's stomach felt sick. He was going to have to go outside, wasn't he? This wasn't just a big joke made up by his dad to scare him.

A blast of cool, 'fresh' air hit Jason in the face. It was like being slapped by nature. It smelled of afternoon sunlight and spring flowers. Everything about it was *awful*.

Jason looked up at his dad.

"But what if I get attacked by a bear and die?" he said.

"In the middle of Charlottesville?" Thomas wrinkled his nose. "It's a risk I'm willing to take." With that, Jason was pushed out, and the red front door closed, inches away from his nose. He was left standing on the front porch.

Jason stroked the brass doorknob, giving it a few experimental turns - just in case – but the door was locked. He heard his dad chuckle on the other side, and walk away. His footsteps vanished into the house. *He probably went back to the kitchen to destroy some more spaghetti,* Jason thought. The nice, warm, indoor kitchen.

"Fine," said Jason to no one in particular. "That's how you want to play it?"

He turned around and sat down on the front step, a new plan forming in his head. Pulling his phone out of his back pocket, Jason grinned. He could play *KNIGHTS OF ZEMBALOR* right here. He didn't need a comfy bed, or sturdy walls or warmth and safety to enjoy his favorite game (although that would have been nice…).

Jason smirked as he opened the app. His dad thought he was *so* smart. He thought he was *so* great. But many knights in Zembalor had thought that too and, like his dad, they had been

DEFEATED by Jason Finn!

The game came to life with the fanfare of electronic trumpets that he was so used to- *Da-daaaaah!*

Jason sighed happily. Man, he was good!

But quick as a flash, his grin disappeared. The screen flashed red, followed by...

(CHECK YOUR INTERNET CONNECTION)

No! Jason clicked and swiped through to the settings on his phone. What he saw filled his body with a cold, crushing terror.

WIFI
Password Incorrect.

Jason looked up. His dad was standing at the nearby window, waving at him. "Have fun!" he mouthed.

The harsh reality sunk in. Jason's dad had *changed the WIFI password.*

"NOOOOOOOOO!" cried Jason.

2. Loading...

Jason had been sitting on the doorstep for seven hundred and thirty-three seconds (he'd counted) when a voice made him look up.

"Hi, Jason. What are you up to?"

It was a deep, rumbling sort of voice, and it belonged to Ben, the boy who lived next door. Ben was standing on the far side of the white, wooden fence that separated the two front yards. He was a tall, muscular boy, three years older than Jason. They'd known each other for as long as Jason could remember, but they didn't talk much these days. Ben, unlike Jason, was much more interested in actual sports than in playing sports on a games console. He was really into football. Or was it basketball? Or maybe soccer? Something with a lot of running and sweating. Just looking at Ben for too long made Jason feel tired. Who would want to spend this much time outside?

Ben leaned on the fence, flipping back his hair from his face so Jason could see his face properly. He looked older than the last time Jason had seen him – his face seemed to have sharper features, and a black sort of fuzz had appeared on his chin. Jason frowned. How long had it been since he had last seen Ben?

"You look a bit down," Ben said.

Jason sighed. "I'm getting fresh air," he said

in a poor imitation of his dad. "I'm living my best life. I'm experiencing the world."

Ben's eyebrows rose. "All that from your doorstep? Impressive."

"I know," Jason said sadly. "I'm so talented."

Ben chuckled. "So how is it going?"

"Well," Jason said, pulling his phone back out of his pocket. "I think I have nearly figured out the new wi-fi password. Dad likes to add random numbers and objects at the end like 'Fish39' or 'Lamp220,' to try and confuse me. But I think if I can figure out what kind of mood he was in when he set it, then…" Jason looked up. Ben was looking at him with a mixture of concern and pity. "Alright, fine." Jason tucked his phone back into his coat pocket. "It's not going very well."

"Yeah, I thought so."

There was a long pause.

"Soooooo…" Jason was beginning to remember why he didn't talk to Ben that much. It got awkward so quickly. Jason grasped for conversation starters (or perhaps a way to get Ben to leave!). "How is the… big game? With the balls?"

Ben laughed. "It's good."

Jason was annoyed. Did Ben not have anything more to say about it? "What are you doing here?"

Ben glanced down the street. "I'm heading out to an event."

"A sporting event?" Jason tried to smile, but his face only managed a pained grimace.

"No, the soccer season doesn't start again for a few more weeks."

Soccer! Ah-ha! He knew it!

"It's an event for my mom's work. They're testing out a new product and want some people to help out."

Ben's mom worked for a technology company, or a computer company, or something like that.

"What new product?"

Ben shrugged. "A new games console, I

think."

Ben had said it so calmly that Jason had to blink a few times before it really set in.

"A – a NEW games console?" he spluttered, standing up and rushing over to the fence. "A brand new, never played before, shiny, exciting, beautiful, out of the box games console?!"

Ben, who towered over Jason when he was this close, looked down at him, confused. Jason realized that in his excitement, he had grabbed the front of Ben's t-shirt. He took a step backward, pretending to brush down his front.

"Um," Ben said. "Yes?"

A new games console... Jason took a breath. This was the stuff of dreams. A chance to be ahead of the trend, of knowing what the future of gaming might look like. Jason needed to come up with a sensible argument as to why Ben should allow him to come along to the event. Maybe he could point out that he was very experienced with games. Or that he was thinking of becoming a streamer. All he knew that he needed to say it calmly, and he needed to be mature about it.

"Takemewithyoutakemewithyoutakemewithy oupleasepleaseplease!" Jason's voice went all squeaky as he spoke.

Another pause followed.

At some point during his outburst, Jason had fallen to his knees. He got up in as dignified a way as possible. "You know," he added. "If you want to."

Smoothly done. There was no way Ben could say no to that.

Ben looked uncomfortable. He looked at the blue plastic watch on his wrist. He was taking an excruciatingly long time to think about it. Jason held his breath. Fourteen centuries went by (maybe more).

"Yeah, alright," Ben said. Jason let out a breath. "If your dad is cool with it."

KNOCK KNOCK KNOCK.

They turned to see Jason's dad's face pressed against the front window of the house, his nose squished. He knocked against the window with his fist, nodding enthusiastically.

"I'm cool with it!" Thomas Finn shouted in a muffled voice. "Go have fun, Jason! Live your life! Experie-" He was cut off by the sound of the fire alarm going off in the kitchen. His eyes widened, and he disappeared from the window.

"Is he okay?" Ben asked.

"It doesn't matter!" Jason said, ushering Ben to the sidewalk. "What does matter is where this event is. How are we getting there?"

Ben chuckled again. "The next bus is in five minutes."

***

The Screaming Howlers roared through Ava Yu's earphones. They were singing her favorite song, perfect for blocking out the world around her. It was called: I'm Sad and Stuff.

"I'm really sad!" the lead singer bellowed like a rampaging elephant. "And for a really good reasoooon..."

The bus slowed down, and Ava opened her eyes. She had chosen a seat at the back of the bus, on the right side: this way, she could watch everyone get on and get off. Two boys were waiting at the next stop; the first one was very tall, muscular and dark-skinned. He moved and talked in a relaxed manner, joking with the bus driver as he stepped inside. The second boy was the complete opposite of the first: small and pale, untidy. His brown hair was an uncontrollable mess, a bit like a hedgehog who would have fallen into a washing machine, and his clothes were at least two sizes too big for him. His eyes twitched nervously as he fumbled with his jean pockets for change, which he dropped on the floor as soon as he pulled it out. Money fluttered to the ground, and he almost shouted an apology, flopping to the ground in an attempt to pick it up.

Ava rolled her eyes.

What was wrong with this boy? The other people on the bus had places to be. More importantly, she had places to be. He was holding everyone up. An old woman nearby even looked up from her knitting to tut and shook her head.

Ava closed her eyes again. There was nothing she could do except listen to the song which was still playing.

"You broke my heaaaaaaaart, and now I am really saaaaaaaaad!"

The guitarist (Ava liked him a lot because he had six different colors in his hair and beautiful eyes that made her feel lighter whenever she saw them) was about to launch into what Ava considered to be the best guitar solo ever in the universe, period. To her horror, it was interrupted by her phone getting a message.

Blingle bloop!

Ava knew who the message was from before she even looked at it.

WHERE R U?!!?!?!

Her older sister, Terri, always liked to overdo the punctuation. Ava tried to ignore the text. Beautiful Eyes was playing.

Blingle bloop!

MOM IS FREEKIN OUT!!!

Blingle bloop!

IT'S BUD.

Blingle bloop!

BAD*

Blingle bl-

REAL BAB.

Blin-

COME HOME!!!!!

Ava would never get to hear Beautiful Eyes' guitar solo at this rate. She typed back a quick reply.

B bck sn.

She clicked send.

"Sad, sad, sad, sad, sad, I'm so sad," the music continued. She had missed the solo. Disappointing. The music was interrupted again.

TERRI YU CALLING

Her phone vibrated aggressively in her hand. Ava rolled her eyes. Why couldn't Terri just leave her alone?

She rejected the call and set her cell phone to airplane mode, blocking all calls and texts. That'd show her. Sure, she was going to be in major trouble when she got home, but she was already in major trouble anyway. How much more major could it get?

Ava opened her email app – double-checking for what felt the thousandth time the email she had received last week.

ARE YOU READY

FOR THE NEXT GENERATION

OF GAMING?

DO YOU WANT

TO BE AHEAD

OF THE GAME?

UP TO DATE WITH

THE LATEST TECH?

COME ALONG

TO TONY'S GAMING STORE

NEXT WEDNESDAY 5 PM

AND SHOW US

WHAT YOU ARE MADE OF!!!!!!

Sponsored by Live Real Co.

Live Real. Play Virtual.

Ava looked at her watch. It was 4.49pm. She would make it, but not as early as she had hoped. If her mom didn't have such *strict rules* about climbing out of windows (and if she hadn't burst into her room unannounced), Ava could have caught the bus *before* this one. She would already be there. She might even have been able to persuade Tony, of Tony's Gaming Store, to let her get a glimpse of the tech before everyone else. Ava and Tony went way back. She bought *all* her games from him.

Why did parents have to make everything so difficult?

The bus slowed down again, and Ava glanced out of the window. They were a block away from Tony's gaming store. She could get off at the next stop. Gathering her things, she got up, waiting for the bus to pull up to the sidewalk.

To her surprise, the two boys who had got on earlier also stood up as though it was their stop. Tall-And-Sporty and Pale-And-Messy. Her lip curled up in annoyance. What if they were also going to the event? She had known she probably wouldn't be the only one to show up, but did it have to be those two? She had a bad feeling about them. Especially the messy one.

Ava shook it off. Even if they were going to the event, it didn't matter. In fact, it made sense. It was a brand-new games console. There would probably be a lot of people there. Her heart sank a little. She would probably have to queue for hours. If only she had escaped from her bedroom earlier!

The bus came to a stop, and Ava kept her distance from the boys as she got off. She looked at her phone, considering playing the song again, but she saw that the boys were talking in front of her. She followed them down the street, listening to their conversation.

"So," Pale-And-Messy said to Tall-And-Sporty, "what kind of console is it?" Bingo, she was right. They were going to the gaming event.

"No idea," Tall-And-Sporty replied.

"What about games? Any idea what games they'll have?" It was a good question.

"Exciting ones, hopefully." But not a good answer.

"Uh… what about…" Pale-And-Messy was running out of steam. "Anything?"

Tall-And-Sporty shrugged.

"Oh."

The conversation died there; they walked on in silence. Did these boys actually know each other? Ava wondered. They didn't seem like very good friends. They reached the end of the block, opposite Tony's Gaming Store. The boys stopped, and Ava quickly knelt down, pretending to tie up her shoelace. She might have been listening to their conversation, but she didn't want to look like a creepy stalker.

"Ben…" Pale-And-Messy said.

"Yeah?" Tall-And-Sporty replied.

"Don't you think that is a bit strange?"

Ava's eyes widened. Were they talking about *her*? Who were they to call *her* strange? *They* were the strange ones! She had the right to be here as much as anyone else.

She had made up her mind to stand up and tell them what she thought of them (Stupid bullies! Stinky boys! Ugly… face… people!) when she looked up and realized they weren't talking about her at all.

They were looking across the street at the store. Ava followed their gaze. Tony's Gaming Store was a staple of Charlottesville. She was sure it had been standing for as long as the city had been there (probably). Any self-respecting gamer in Charlottesville bought everything from Tony's – it always had the best deals, and Tony always had a story and a smile.

Except for today.

Today, Tony's store was locked up tighter than a safe. Heavy padlocks hung on the shutters, and the place looked abandoned.

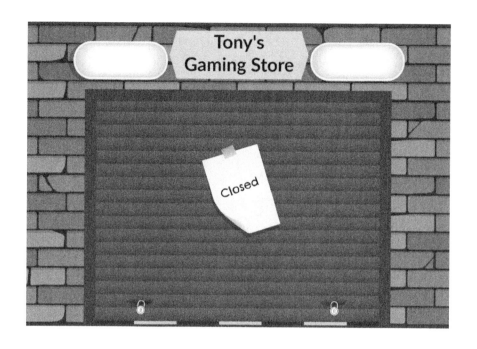

Tony's Gaming Store was
CLOSED.

3. NEW GAME

"Don't you think that's a bit strange?" Jason asked as he looked across the street. Tony's was *closed*. Today, of all the days in the entire span of history? Had Ben got the date wrong? Would Jason have to go back to sitting on the front doorstep?

Questions whizzed through his head like a tornado on a sugar high. Ben, however, looked as calm as ever. He just shrugged. "It's unusual."

UNUSUAL? Jason thought. More like a disaster of *epic* proportions! Had he left the comforts of his home for this? Standing on the street in front of a closed shop? It was possibly the worst-case scenario (assuming aliens didn't turn up in the next few seconds to try to eat his brain, but with the way today was going, anything was possible).

Ben crossed the road and Jason slumped after him (while keeping an eye out for aliens.) As they got close to the store, Jason's worst fears were confirmed: the place was dead. No friendly Tony waiting to greet them. No shelves of games lining the walls. Just harsh metallic shutters, hiding whatever was inside, which Jason assumed was more disappointment. Or aliens.

Ben flicked one of the heavy padlocks holding the shutters down with his hand. It went *clunk*.

Ben chuckled. "Well, this is a problem."

"No kidding!" said Jason.

"What do *you* think we should do?"

Jason opened his mouth to answer and noticed that Ben wasn't talking to him. Ben was talking to a girl who had just appeared out of nowhere and was now standing a few meters from them. She was about the same height as Jason, dressed in scruffy jeans with holes in them and a pink t-shirt. Her 'scruffy rebellious' look was, however, slightly dampened by her neatly trimmed, shoulder-length black hair. She looked up from her phone, her steely gray eyes wide.

"*Agh*!" Jason jumped. "Where did *you* come from?"

(Was she an alien?)

"I was on the same bus as you," she said dryly. "I've been right behind you for the last few minutes."

Jason frowned. Had she? He didn't remember seeing her.

Ben chuckled. "Hey," he said. "You're Terri's sister, right? Ava?"

The girl, Ava, rolled her eyes. "Yeah. Don't remind me."

"I'm Ben," he said. "This is Jason."

"Charmed," Ava said, looking at Jason through narrowed eyes.

"You're here for the event too, Ana?" Jason asked.

"It's *AVA*. And yes. Although we are either early or…" she peered into the shop. "…way too late."

Ben kicked the shutter, making the whole place rattle. "Maybe there is another way in?"

Ava snorted. "Other than the front door? What kind of event is this?"

It didn't make sense for there to be a back door, but Jason was so eager to play on this new console that he would have tried anything.

"I'll go have a look!" he said and set off around the corner of the street. It was a breath of fresh air, being momentarily alone again, apart from the other people walking along the sidewalk, of course.

Or the cars driving by.

At least he didn't need to talk to them.

Boy, did he miss his room.

Maybe, he decided, it was best to focus on the task at hand. As soon as he went to the event, and experienced awesome gaming awesomeness, he could go home and never talk to Amy or Ben or anyone else again. He could go back to being a Knight in *ZEMBALORE!*

Between the gaming store and the next shop, which seemed to sell soap, was an alleyway which - yes! - led to the back of the store, where a green door stood. The only problem was a chain-link fence that lined the alley, blocking their way.

Jason turned to tell Ben.

"Hey B- *Agh!*" Jason leaped back.

Standing next to him was the girl again,

staring into the alley.

"Hey Ben," she said. "There's a door here."

"I was going to say that!" Jason snapped.

She grinned at him. "It's not a competition, *James.*"

"It's *Jason*," Jason hissed. He felt the heat rise up in his cheeks. She just wanted to make him look stupid! He took a slow breath.

"You're right," he said. "It's not a competition." He looked up at the fence, judging the distance. "BUT I'M GOING TO GET THERE FIRST!"

"What?" said Ava.

Jason didn't reply. He was too busy running up to the fence, grabbing the chain links between his fingers and *puuuuuullling* himself up….

(Were fences always this big?)

… puuulling…. himseeeelf…

(Phew, maybe he needed to get out more.)

*Puuuuulling hiiiimseeeelf **uuuuuup**…*

(Yes! He was climbing!)

Ava snorted out a laugh from the sidewalk. "Seriously?" she asked.

Jason was halfway up now. He could *taste* the victory. His fingers burned, and his back creaked like an old ship, but he was going to show this Ava girl what was up!

Ava sighed. "This is stupid," she said.

Jason didn't think it was stupid. More like *genius*. He was a fingers-width away from the top of the fence. He was going to –

The whole fence shook and rattled. Jason glanced sideways. Ava was pulling herself up the fence as well!

The race was on!

(His back *really* hurt now. Maybe this was why people didn't climb fences…)

By the time he had pulled himself over the top, Jason was sweating. Every intake of breath didn't seem to have enough oxygen in it. His heart went *ba-doom ba-doom* in his ears.

Still, he managed to get his leg over the metal bar. He was almost on the other side.

But Ava (Jason was pretty sure she was snarling) was pulling her leg over the top of the fence too! How was she so fast?

Soon they were both precariously perched on the top, like two fledglings about to take their first trip out of the nest. They stared at each other, angrily.

Ben appeared around the far corner of the building and went right up to the green door. *How had he got to the other side of the fence?* He looked at the two of them, tilting his head slightly to the side.

"Uh," he said. "What are you doing?"

"We're –" Ava said breathlessly.

WOAH!

Whatever balance Jason had…suddenly disappeared. He tumbled towards Ben and could do nothing as the floor suddenly came towards him rapidly.

Jason hit the side of a trash can and bounced onto the concrete below.

"Ouch!"

The world around him went all fuzzy as hot pain blossomed across his back. Jason didn't want to open his eyes, just in case the damage was serious. Maybe he could just crack an eye open… *yes, it was alright, maybe?*

He had cut the palm of his hand, but nothing serious.

Ben towered over him, a dark shadow against the bright sky.

"Are you OK?" his voice rumbled over the sound of traffic. Another dark figure joined him in looking down at Jason.

"I touched the door first." It was Ava, but she spoke in a small voice and didn't meet his eye. "What hurts?"

"My… everything…" Jason wheezed in a little voice.

Ben pulled him to his feet. Something in his back went *click* and Jason winced, but he seemed to be able to stand.

"Wait," Jason said, rubbing his elbow. "How did you get here without climbing over the fence?"

Ben pointed behind him. "I came from the other side. There is no fence blocking the alley there."

Jason looked in that direction. There was *another entrance. WITHOUT A FENCE.* He turned back to Ava.

She shrugged. "We got here in one piece." She scratched her nose. "More or less…"

Ben reached up to knock on the door of the shop, but it swung open before he could. A very thin woman stared at them through narrowed eyes. Her hair was long and gray, and she wore a smart-looking business suit.

The way she looked at them made Jason feel like a dead worm that she had just discovered in her salad.

"You're late," she snapped.

4. Tutorial

Thirty-two minutes earlier...

"You're early!" said the smartly-dressed woman.

Frankie stared up at her and felt a familiar tightening in his throat. He wasn't good at what his sister called 'communicating like a normal human being.' People spoke so fast, and so loudly. He often found it hard to focus on what was going on, never mind come up with a good answer.

He looked at his sister, Brittany, for support.

She was holding her phone over her head, trying to take a selfie, but frowned, tutted and tried a different spot in the back alley.

OK, thought Frankie.

You can do this.
You're eight-and-a-quarter years old!
Almost an adult.

He opened his mouth to speak.

"............"

The woman at the door held her smile, but it had too many teeth, and her smile didn't reach her cold brown eyes.

"Excuse me?" she asked.

Brittany sighed, flicking her blonde hair to the side. She shoved her phone into her pocket. "He said, 'We are here to try out the new games console.'" Brittany punched him in the shoulder. "He never speaks loud enough."

"I see," said the cold-eyed woman. "Follow me. You've still got half an hour until we start."

Frankie was about to follow her inside when Brittany grabbed his arm, spinning him around.

"Half an hour?" she whispered. "You said we were going to be late!"

"……. .. …..," said Frankie.

"I do **NOT** take that long to get ready!" Brittany snapped.

She would have said more, but her phone vibrated, and she had to look at it. Frankie sighed and walked into the shop.

The back room of the shop was a mess, but it was the *best* kind of a mess. Games, new and old, were stacked in piles almost as high as Frankie. They seemed to be bursting out of the walls as if the shop itself was made of games. In one corner, there was a stack of brand-new consoles, the *Xtreme Boxatron 3*, if Frankie wasn't mistaken. They were untouched, seals unbroken. Frankie took off his glasses and wiped them with his shirt. Was this real? He still had a *Boxatron 1* at home, and even that was second-hand from Brittany. This was like walking through a dream.

They moved into the main part of the store. Frankie gasped. It looked nothing like what he was used to. All the gaming merchandise, posters, games, consoles, t-shirts, toys, had been pushed to the sides of the room and were covered up by a thick, translucent plastic material that hung down from the ceiling. The checkout desk usually came with a friendly Tony standing behind it, who waved at Frankie whenever he entered, but today the table was covered in very complex computer equipment which beeped and flashed. There was a computer screen with lines of letters and numbers scrolling across it. Behind it, all was a group of adults, huddled together and talking in hushed voices. They all wore white lab coats, like scientists in those sci-fi movies Brittany made him watch. The group glanced at them as they entered, and their conversation seemed to take a very serious and intense tone.

The woman cleared her throat and gestured towards the center of the room, where five chairs, each a different color, waited. They looked like the big office chair that Frankie's dad had beside his desk at home, except without the wheels – and wires connected these to the computers on the desk. Frankie wouldn't be spinning around in these.

"Please choose a chair and get comfy," the woman said. "We hopefully won't have to wait long until our other guests arrive."

Frankie skittered over to the furthest left chair – the yellow one – before the woman could do anything horrifying…like start up a conversation.

Brittany sighed, put her phone back into her pocket, and sat down in the green chair next to him.

"…. … …?" asked Frankie.

"No, I don't know who else is coming," Brittany replied.

***

"You're late." The woman was standing in the doorway and scowled at Ben.

He shrugged. "Sorry, the bus was a bit slow."

There was a tense second where Jason thought they wouldn't be let in. The woman finally tore her gaze away from Ben and looked at Ava and Jason.

"Welcome," she said, a smile forcing its way

onto her face. "Please, follow me."

As they walked through the backroom of Tony's Gaming Store (oh, the games! The thousands and thousands of games! Was that a brand-new edition of Captain Amazing? Would anyone notice if he slipped it into his pocket?) the woman talked to them, gesturing this way and that, but not looking at them at all.

"My name is Melissa Turnbout. I am the representative of Live Real Co. who is very kindly running this event today. You'll be testing one of our brand-new products."

A rush of excitement surged through Jason's body. "The new games console?"

Melissa turned and did another of those forced-smiles. "Yes, one of those," she said and opened the slightly worn, red door into the main store.

Both Jason and Ava gasped. This wasn't Tony's Gaming Store! It was like something out of a sci-fi movie. Wires and blinking lights linked up to five very comfy-looking chairs in the center of the room. Two were already taken up. Where were the games? Where was Tony?

One of the two kids already seated in the chairs was a small boy. He was maybe seven or eight. He stared at the room through round glasses, his blue eyes very big. The chair made him look even smaller. He hadn't taken off his puffy red coat and seemed very nervous.

Next to him was a girl, older, who seemed unfazed (and unimpressed) by the futuristic set-up of the room. She was very tall and thin, her frizzy blonde hair falling down either side of her face. She stared at the phone in her hands, occasionally biting one of her nails with her two very large front teeth. She glanced up, saw Ben, and waved. He waved back and wandered over to her, striking up a cheerful conversation.

In fact, Ben chatted with other people in the room, including Melissa and the group of lab-coat-wearing adults who were working on something behind the chairs. He seemed to know everyone. They seemed to like him.

Jason suddenly felt very alone. Maybe he didn't need to try out a new games console after all...

"The chairs," Ava said next to him.

"Huh?" he said.

"The chairs are the games console," she said. "Must be some sort of virtual reality thing."

They were both standing in the doorway still – neither of them daring to take a step forward into the room. Ava kicked something on the floor.

Melissa spun on her toes and faced them. "Alright," she said, clapping her hands together. "Please choose a chair, and then we can *finally*," she glanced at Ben, "begin."

Jason knew instantly which chair he would go for. In the center of the group was a sleek black chair which gleamed in the dim light of the store. Everything about it screamed *awesome gamer*, and he knew that whoever sat in that chair-

He was so busy staring in wonder that when Ava pushed past him and sat in the black chair, he did not react fast enough. Before he could open his mouth to protest, Ava had turned away from him and waved to the girl next to her. "Hello," she said. "I'm Ava."

"Brittany," the girl replied. "This is Frankie."

Frankie blinked.

Reluctantly, Jason slumped down into the brown chair next to Ava's. Brown was a stupid color. Why couldn't he have the black chair? The remaining blue chair was taken by Ben, who chuckled as he sat down.

"This is going to be interesting," Ben said. "I wonder how they have compensated for the vertical pressure drift problems they were having."

"The what, huh, what?" Jason asked.

Ben shook his head. "I'll tell you later."

Melissa nodded at the scientists, and Jason felt his heart begin to beat wildly in his chest. This was it! He was at the gaming event. They were about to experience something that no one else had before. It almost didn't feel real.

"Thank you for coming," Melissa said. "You five are going to be the first to test the brand new Live Real Co. LivePods! A virtual life simulator."

The boy called Frankie raised a small hand.

"Yes?" asked Melissa.

"……. ….?"

Jason couldn't hear a word the boy said. His lips were moving, but only the tiniest of sounds were coming out.

"Uuuuh," Melissa replied.

"He said," Brittany spoke up reluctantly, "what is a virtual life simulator?"

Melissa smiled a shark-like grin. "You're about to find out." She clicked her fingers.

The scientist-adults sprang into action. Jason felt something heavy being placed on his head, and clips were attached around his chin. It was like he was wearing a bike helmet, only a bit *more*. It made his skull tingle. A strange clicking and whirring sound came from somewhere above him. Jason tried to look up but found his head was stuck in place.

A cold, clammy hand grabbed onto his left wrist and squeezed tightly. He looked down as far as he could.

Was that… Ava? Grabbing his wrist?

It suddenly felt very warm under the helmet.

"Just relax and let our technicians do their work," Melissa grinned. She looked over them and nodded. A particularly hairy man in a messy lab coat whispered something in her ear. Her grin widened. "Ok, we are all set," she said. "Enjoy yourselves!"

Ava's hand let go of his wrist and raised into

the air.

"Wait!!" Jason heard Ava shout. "What are we supposed to do?"

Melissa waved her question away. "You'll find out."

"Is this going to hurt?" Jason blurted out.

Melissa looked at him with piercing brown eyes. "I hope not."

"You ho-?" Jason didn't manage to finish his sentence. The world around him seemed to crack and melt, Melissa's brown eyes shattering like glass and falling away like water. He was left in darkness.

All sound stopped, and a voice boomed out of nowhere:

"LIVE REAL CO. LIVE REAL.

PLAY VIRTUAL!"

Jason tried to scream, but no sound came out.

The world went bright white.

5. Choose Your Character

The sky above him was bright blue. He lay on his back and stared up at a little cloud that floated by. The cloud reminded him of an octopus – no… a rabbit with five ears and the tail of a snake.

Or maybe it was an ice-cream.

"Hello, little ice-cream cloud," mumbled Jason.

Wait!

Hadn't he been indoors a few seconds ago?

Jason's mind was a jumble of words and pictures. Everything popped up in no particular order. *Charlottesville. Gaming. LiveReal. Spaghetti. Ava.*

That last word made him shiver, but he wasn't sure why.

Suddenly, the blue sky with its ice cream cloud was blocked out by a large shadow. It looked down on his small form, and then said: **"Moo."**

Jason blinked. It was a cow. A cow with wings and it was towering over him. It was black, with large splotches of white on its side. It blinked at him with big, cow eyelashes.

Why was there a cow in Tony's Gaming Store?

Jason sat up.

Why was Tony's Gaming Store a grassy field?!

"Moo," said the cow again. It prodded the side of his head with its big, wet nose. Jason looked around. He was *definitely* not in the gaming store. He wasn't even in Charlottesville. He was in a field. Outside. With a cow.

In the distance, he could make out the edge of a forest, and beyond that, a large white-topped mountain range that reached into the sky. He seemed to be in some sort of valley.

How long had he been unconscious? Had he managed to sleep-walk all the way to Switzerland?

"HeLloOo?" he said and winced. The sound of his own voice crashed against the inside of his skull.

"Oh wow, that's impressive!"

Jason recognized the voice. Ben was sitting up in the field next to him, although Jason didn't remember noticing him before.

"Oh, wow." He turned and looked at Jason. "Jason? Oh, wow!"

"Oh, wow?" said Jason, feeling a little dumb.

"**Moo?**" said the cow.

"Ugh, my head." Suddenly Ava was also sitting up in the grass, opposite Jason. She held her hands over the sides of her head, as though her brain was about to fall out of her ears. "Where are we?" She squinted in the sunlight. "Have we been kidnapped?"

"Oh, what a view!" Brittany said from the other side of the cow – peeking through its legs. "Great spot for a selfie. Oh, and everyone is here!"

Ben laughed loudly. "Don't you get it? This is *it!*"

"*It?*" Jason scratched his head. "What is *it*?"

"*The GAME!*" grinned Ben. "We are inside the game! The LivePod!"

Jason looked around. This *couldn't* be the

game. They were *outside*. There was a cow. *A cow!* He could feel the breeze on his face. He could feel the warmth of the sun above him. He could-

Jason sniffed.

He could *smell* the cow. (Ew.)

"Moo," said the cow. It looked offended.

There was too much going on, and a slight ringing still echoing in his ears. Jason closed his eyes and opened them again.

Yes, definitely a field. Grass. Cow. *Spaghetti.* No, wait, that last one was wrong.

As the cow wandered away, Jason could see that all five of them were sitting in a circle. Even the small boy, Frankie, was there, sitting next to Brittany and scratching his head.

"Um, if we are in the game, what are we supposed to *do*?" said Brittany. "Like, where is the map or the tutorial or whatever?"

"……..," said Frankie.

"Yeah, my head hurts too. I can taste toothpaste," Brittany groaned. "Can anyone else taste toothpaste?"

Ava got to her feet and stretched. "This is so weird," she said. "I've played VR games before, but this feels a little less virtual and a little more…"

"Real," grinned Ben. "LiveReal, am I right?"

"I guess," said Ava. "So, do we wander around, or…"

Jason stood up. The world around him spun slightly, and he grabbed for the nearest thing to balance himself.

The thing was soft and squishy and a little bit sticky. It said: **"Moo!"** Jason looked up. His hand was resting on the cow's nose, and the cow was looking directly at him.

"Uh…" he said.

The cow's eyes flashed bright white.

Jason's eyes widened.

"I've never seen a cow do that before," Brittany whispered.

The light spread across the cow's face and over its body until the whole cow was just a shining beacon of light in the middle of the field.

"Impressive lighting effects," said Ben, nudging Jason with his arm.

Jason was too busy squinting at the glowing cow to answer. *What was going on?*

Then…

Jason raised his hands instinctively to his face, but instead of being thrown off his feet, or burned to a crisp, the light just… disappeared, along with the cow.

Standing in the cow's place was a purple-skinned woman, dressed in a long red robe. She looked at them through bright green eyes and smiled. The smile, however, didn't reach her eyes.

Jason frowned. She looked a bit like… Melissa?

Purple Melissa reached into her pocket and held out her hand. Resting on her palm were five colored stones, each about the size of a golf ball. They were the same colors as the chairs they had sat on in the store.

"Choose your destiny," she said in a soft voice. "Then, we can begin."

Brittany had never been in a game like this. In fact, the more she thought about it, the more she realized she had never actually been *inside* a game. They were usually just on her phone screen, like the game *Pobble Pop* or *Square Explosion*. They didn't have fields and cows and purple ladies (though *Pobble Pop* did have a purple cat). Brittany found the whole thing quite confusing.

It might have been fun if she didn't have to drag around Frankie. Her half-brother had the amazing ability to ruin *everything*. It was just a matter of time.

Frankie turned to her and said, "…. … …… …!"

Brittany rolled her eyes. "It's alright," she said. "You can take a rock. She's not a stranger. Look, it's Melissa! Purple Melissa!"

What was wrong with him? Thinking about *stranger danger* at a time like this?

".. ….. ….?"

"I know we don't really know her," Brittany stamped her foot. "Look, if you don't want to take a rock, you can just sit here in this field on your own. You won't even have a cow for company, because it exploded, thanks to him." She waved her arm in the direction of the pale boy. What was his name, Jack? Jason?

"Hey!" said Jack-Jason, his cheeks flushing in

embarrassment.

"Sorry," Brittany said. (It was true though. He had made the cow explode. Brittany made a mental note never to touch a cow's nose in the future.)

Ava was the first to step up and take a rock. She picked the black one, the same as the chair she had chosen, and held in front of her face, examining it.

"Now what?" said Ava.
Purple Melissa turned to Ava, her green eyes piercing, and said:

"SHADOW."

Ava opened her mouth to reply when suddenly…

She was gone! Just like the cow!

Brittany screamed, grabbing onto Frankie. Maybe he wasn't wrong about the rocks!

But then, in the length of a breath, Ava was back, standing exactly where she was before. Only her clothes were completely different! Her jeans were replaced with black tights and a baggy gray skirt. Over her chest she had thick black armor with two sharp knives attached. Her shoes were replaced with black heavy boots.

Ava looked down at herself.

"Woah!" she said. "Look at me!"

"Woah," said Brittany. "It's like one of those make-over shows you see on TV, except instead of looking like a princess, you look –" Brittany paused. "Well, kind of the same but with a lot of manly-looking leather."

"You've picked your character!" grinned Ben. "Quick, everyone, grab a rock!"

Ben reached out and grabbed the blue stone.

Melissa turned to him again.

"STRENGTH."

Ben was gone. Brittany remembered not to scream this time. Frankie glanced up at her again.

".......?" he asked.

"It doesn't *look* like it hurts," Brittany said, but she was also a bit worried about exploding.

Ben came back. He was dressed in shining silver armor, a sword, and shield in his hands, his eyes wide.

"Woah," said Jason. "You're a *knight*!"

"I'm a knight?!" Ben seemed shocked and impressed. He swung his sword dramatically in front of him.

CLANG!

It fell to the floor, landing on the ground.

"Oops," he grinned. "I guess I need some

practice."

Brittany didn't want to waste any more time. "Come on, Frankie," she said. "Let's grab a stone."

"......."

"Oh, stop complaining," she said. "It's just a game!"

She grabbed the green stone from Melissa's hand. It felt weirdly warm as if it was alive. Brittany looked down, confused. Where was the explosion? Maybe her stone was broken? She was about to ask

–

"LIFE."

She didn't feel like she had disappeared. Everyone was just suddenly looking at her. "What?" she said, looking at herself.

The stone was no longer in her hand; instead, she had a golden bow. She was also wearing a long robe made from leaves and pink flowers. On her back was a leather quiver, filled with golden arrows. She did a little spin. Petals fluttered down from her dress. She grinned.

"I could get used to this," she said.

"PROTECTION."

She hadn't even seen Frankie pick the stone.

For the briefest of seconds, Brittany was worried he wouldn't come back. How would she explain it to his mom? "Sorry, I lost Frankie in a game when he exploded after taking a rock from a lady."

Yeah, that made *perfect* sense.

Then he was back. He was back and dressed in a brown robe which made him look even smaller than before. He had a long, wooden staff with a deep purple gem at the top. It glowed in the sunlight.

Frankie looked up at Brittany and said: "..... ....?"

"No, I don't want to swap, you weirdo!" Brittany said.

It was Jason's turn. He looked *very* excited. "I can't *wait* to see what I look like!" he said. He grabbed the brown and final stone left in Melissa's hand and waited.

"CHOSEN," said Melissa.

When he came back, Brittany burst out laughing.

6. Level One

It was a *disaster*. A complete, utter, devastating
DISASTER.

This was meant to be the most epic gaming
experience of his life. He had been chosen – quite
literally – by the game. Purple-Melissa had said
CHOSEN. He hadn't misheard. When someone
says **CHOSEN**, it's not unreasonable to expect your
character to be a knight, or a wizard, or a ranger. Or
even some kind of giant dragon-monster with fifty
heads, each spitting a different color of fire or acid.

It didn't have to be a giant dragon-monster.
He would have been happy with a little one.

But no. Instead, he got this: his clothes turned
into itchy, beige cotton top and pants, stained with
mud (*please* let it just be mud!) that stank like it had
never even heard of water, never mind soap. And
what was the epic weapon clutched in his hands? A
spade.

A SPADE! Not even a brand-new spade. It
was rusty! No sword and shield. No staff of power.
No. He got *garden tools*. Then he found what he
thought was a knife in a sheath tied around his
waist, but it was blunt, more like a digging tool.

To make it even better, that Brittany girl was laughing her head off so much that she almost choked.

"WHAT IS THIS?" he cried out. "WHERE IS MY COOL GEAR?!"

Ben chuckled. "Ouch," he said. "You pulled the short straw, I think."

"I don't know," grinned Ava. "I think it suits him."

Jason turned to her, eyes filled with fire, but he was interrupted by Purple-Melissa.

"You have all chosen your destiny. Now prepare yourselves for a **great journey.** I fear it will be long and dangerous."

"Oh," said Brittany. "That doesn't sound like fun. Are there shorter, less dangerous journeys we can take?"

Ava grinned. "I think it's going to be awesome."

Purple-Melissa swept her arm dramatically in front of her. The image of a castle appeared in the air between them.

"The evil sorceress, **Betrayna,** has struck
again. This time, she has used her dark powers to
strike at the heart of the kingdom of Realopia!"

With a complex hand gesture, the castle
morphed and twisted in the air. A darkened sky
loomed over it, and the stone walls were black with
fire. "The King and his heirs...are dead."

"Aw," said Brittany. "That's sad."

Jason raised a hand. "Hi, yes, sorry, I just
wanted to ask why I have a spade and not like, a
crossbow or something?" He waved his spade

through the floating castle. The castle wobbled a bit, like jello.

"But," Melissa continued, her brown eyes flaring with magical power. "All is not lost. For there is another who can overthrow her."

"That's great, but about my spade –" Jason said again.

Melissa turned to him. Jason stepped back instinctively.

"I think you need to let her finish," Ben whispered. Jason held his tongue – for now.

"There is one here with the **blood of kings**," she said. "They can claim the throne and restore order. That person is named –" she raised a finger, her long fingernail painted black. *"PLAYER THREE."* Her voice was strangely robotic. She was pointing directly at Jason.

"Of course," Ben said, his eyes lighting up. "You're CHOSEN, Jason. You're the CHOSEN ONE!"

Jason didn't feel chosen. He felt like a smelly boy with a spade. Chosen to be lame, more like.

Jason glanced over at Ava. She bit her lip, trying not to laugh. Jason looked away.

"Guardians," the woman said. "Your mission is to guide PLAYER THREE to the king's castle in Completia. There you will face *Betrayna* and defeat her, or the world will fall to darkness."

The castle wobbled out of existence, replaced by the laughing face of a woman with sharp features and a thick, twisted grin with sharp fangs protruding from her mouth.

"Ohhh, I like her hair," said Brittany.

Everyone looked at her.

"What? Just because she's evil, doesn't mean I can't appreciate her sense of fashion," she added.

"Your quest," Melissa said, pointing behind her, "begins there, in the dark wood. But be careful. Betrayna's minions lurk everywhere! Good luck!"

Ben raised his hand. "I have a question."

Purple Melissa was gone in a puff of greenish smoke that smelled like pop-tarts.

Ben frowned. "Alright, I guess I don't have a question."

"But we do have A QUEST!" Jason,

surprisingly, felt himself bubbling with excitement.
They were all in the game! They had a mission!
Only he could save the country from Evil… Was it
Bettina? "And I am the CHOSEN ONE!" He waved
his spade in the air in front of him.

Ben chuckled. "Don't let it go to your head."

Frankie was tugging on his sister's sleeve. She
shook him off. "What?" she snapped.

"… …… …" Jason still couldn't hear a word
the little boy said.

"Oh," said Brittany, her face going pale.

"What?" asked Jason. "What did he say?"

"He asked, 'Where's Ava?'" Brittany replied.

Frankie was right.

Somewhere between the start of Purple-
Melissa's speech and Frankie's question, Ava had
disappeared.

***

Ava was standing at the edge of a dark forest,
peering into the trees. When she played games, she
never watched the cut-scenes. Those silly little clips
just stopped her from doing what she wanted to do:
actually playing the game.

She wanted ACTION, not a conversation. She
wanted to test out these scary-looking knives!

As soon as Purple-Melissa had started talking
about kings and castles and blah blah blah, Ava had
started walking. She got the idea. Defeat the bad

guy, win the game. It had been that way since before the first Super Mario game, and that was surely released, like, sometime in the early 1800s.

The group hadn't even noticed her sneaking off. Ava knew that she was more of a solo act, anyway. She could figure out how to play this game all by herself. Ava the *shadow*. It had a nice ring to it.

Now, which way am I supposed to go?

She had hoped for an easily laid out path, but there was none.

Nor was there a nice big arrow telling her where to go, as with most games nowadays. No, all that she could see was a dark forest, and trees with thick, dark trunks that reached far, far up into the sky. Smaller branches twisted out of them like clawing hands, all wrapping around each other. They formed such a thick canopy that very little light got through, giving the forest a dark and mysterious feel. You might even have said it was *spooky*.

No, not spooky. More like stupid, Ava told herself. She had played lots of horror games with her sister, so she wasn't going to freak out or anything.

Ava stepped into the forest. There was a soft crunch of dead leaves under her feet. Forward, she decided, was the best direction to go in. Away from the purple lady and the other weirdos. She'd probably hit the castle eventually; how big could this game be?

The walk, however, wasn't as easy as Ava thought. She had to step over roots, duck under branches, go up and down because the ground was so uneven. Surprisingly, she soon found herself quite tired. She stopped and sighed. At the moment, this felt less like a game and more like those 'nature walks' her parents forced her family to go on every summer. This time, though, she couldn't even listen to music as she walked.

She thought back to Beautiful Eyes and his guitar solo. That's what this game needed — more heavy metal.

She'd even cope with some of that pop stuff her sister liked. Just SOMETHING. It was so boring and quiet.

Ava kicked at a dried pile of mud and slumped down onto a tree stump.

What kind of game was this, anyway? Where were the collectibles? The map? The action and explosions?

Something clicked in her head.

A menu! Surely the game had a main menu. Maybe she could play with the settings? There might even be a map to tell her where to go.

But how could she open a menu without a controller?

Ah-ha! She thought. *Maybe it's voice-activated, like my phone?*

"Menu, open!" she said in a loud, clear voice. Like everything else in the forest, her voice felt dampened and quiet.

"Unlock menu?" she tried.

"Open settings…"

"Hey, Siri?"

"GAME MENU! OPEN FOR ME, I COMMAND YOU!"

The forest sat and watched her. The boring forest. The boring game forest. It continued to be a forest. The trees continued to be trees. Ava continued to be alone - which was good because now she felt a little foolish for yelling at nothing.

Well, she would just keep walking. The sooner she reached the castle, the better, she decided — no point in hanging around in this dreary forest.

The forest watched her go.

7. NEVER SPLIT THE PARTY

Why couldn't the game have been about driving fast cars? Or taking long naps? Jason thought. *Why did I have to do some much running? I hate running!* He let out a long sigh.

Everything was fine until they had entered the forest to look for Ava. It was big and dark and spooky, but that was no big deal. Jason had seen bigger and scarier forests on TV.

They had walked a bit; Ben had let Jason hold his sword and Jason had *almost* convinced him to swap it with his spade but **spoiler alert:** a sword is one *thousand* times cooler than a spade, so Ben politely declined.

Then the wolves appeared.

Wolves, in general, are very dangerous, but these weren't your average every-day wolves, oh no.

Imagine a car. A BIG car. But instead of a bonnet, it has teeth. Instead of windows, it has large, hungry eyes that glisten in the dark. Instead of wheels, it has paws as big as your head with long, sharp claws. Also, it is all covered in fur and shaped like a wolf.

THAT was what these wolves looked like.

They.
Were.
HUGE.

So now they were running. Running through the dark forest, with a pack of snarling beasts stalking after them. Jason bounced over roots and ducked under branches, desperately trying to keep up with Ben, Brittany, and Frankie, who always seemed to be at least ten steps ahead of him.

AWOOOOOOOOOOOOO!

Behind him, something howled. Something big. Jason could guess what it was. His legs burned, and his lungs felt tight in his chest.

He ran faster. Ben's armor flashed in the distance. His shiny knight's armor. *I wish I had some armor,* thought Jason. *I bet that would keep me safe.* He was running faster than ever before (which was not hard, because running was not an activity he ever practiced for fun). He saw Ben getting closer. Jason was catching up! Maybe he wasn't so bad at this running thing, after all!

Ben suddenly stopped.

CLANG!

Jason ran nose-first into Ben's armor. It wasn't so shiny on closer inspection.

"Oowwwww!" Jason groaned, grabbing his nose.

Ben turned, a smile dancing on his lips. "Sorry, Jason," he whispered. "But look!"

Jason had been so busy running that he hadn't bothered to take in the forest around him. Ben had led the group into a small dip in the ground, underneath some thick roots which formed a sort of ceiling above them. Frankie huddled behind Brittany, who was gently poking the roots above them with her bow.

It was dark under here, and it concealed them almost entirely from the wolves in the woods around them!

"I think if we stay quiet, we can lose them,"

Ben whispered.

"We should have played dead," said Brittany. "That's what they say to do on TV!"

".. ... ..." said Frankie.

"Oh, that's grizzly bears, is it? Well, maybe it works with wolves too."

"... ..."

"I don't see *you* coming up with any better ideas." Brittany sighed. "I didn't realize this game would have quite so much running. I'd have worn better shoes."

".. .... .."

"Shh!" said Brittany, "the wolves will hear you!"

They were standing in the dark. The trees creaked overhead. Jason's heart pounded in his ears. His chest rose and fell as he tried to calm his breathing. His body *really* didn't like running. Why couldn't they have just walked calmly away from the wolves? That might have worked. All this running probably got them excited.

"Could you stop breathing so loudly?" Ben whispered to Jason.

"Maybe…it's…you…" Jason said between breaths. Unlikely, of course. With all the sports Ben did, this was probably just another day for him.

Frankie tugged on Ben's sleeve and pointed to the clearing above them.

A large, gray wolf, fur tangled and coarse, stalked around, sniffing the ground and trees nearby. It was hunting for them. A low growl rattled from its throat.

Jason squeaked.

Ben slowly drew his sword, wincing as the metal *screeeeched* against the scabbard. He held it out in front of him.

"OK," he whispered. "This is how it's going to go. When the wolf gets close, I am going to hit it on the nose with this sword, and then we are going to run back to the field."

"More running?" groaned Jason. "Can't we do anything else?"

"We could get eaten by wolves," Brittany said quietly. "Do you think that would be more fun?"

Jason grimaced. "Fine," he said. "More running."

The wolf stopped by the trunk of a tree on the far side of the clearing. It seemed very interested in what it could smell there.

"It's distracted!" Jason whispered.

"OK, new plan," Ben said, excitement in his voice. "Let's sneak that way and –"

"....!"

"Another wolf!" hissed Brittany, pointing to the right. This one seemed bigger. Its fur was a dark brown, and it was heading straight towards them, its dark blue eyes filled with hunger!

"Brittany, use your arrows!" Ben said.

"Oh, right," Brittany said. She fumbled behind her, trying to reach for a golden arrow from her quiver, but in the cramped space, she couldn't pull it out. She twisted and turned, sighing loudly. "It's stuck!" she hissed.

Jason tried to help her, reaching towards the quiver, but Brittany turned at the wrong moment, and Jason fell backward. Grabbing for something to hold on to, he pulled on the quiver. All the arrows tipped out onto the floor!

As they rattled and tinkled to the ground, Jason winced. Both wolves looked in their direction and started to growl louder.

"Oh, no," Brittany said.

"I'll admit, that may have been a little bit my fault," Jason said.

AWOOOOOOOOOOOOOOOOOOOOOOOOOOOO!

Both wolves charged!

There was nowhere they could run. All they could do was stand and wait for the inevitable crunch of jaws on bones.

Frankie stepped forward. He closed his eyes and held his staff out in front of him. The purple stone on top of the staff began to glow.

"What's that?" asked Brittany. She began to say something else, but it was drowned out by a humming noise.

A bright purple light pulsed out of the top of Frankie's staff.

KATHOOOOOOOOOM!

For a second, all that Jason could smell, taste, and see was purple. It reminded him a little of toothpaste mixed with jello.

He blinked. He blinked again. Slowly, the forest returned to its original darkness. The wolves bounced away, yelping like little puppies.

Frankie stared wide-eyed at his staff.

"Woah," said Ben.

"Double woah," agreed Jason.

Brittany hit her brother on the shoulder. "Why didn't you tell us you had **SUPERPOWERS**?" she said. "We wouldn't have had to do all that running!"

"... ….. …?"

"How could you not know something like that?!"

Ben chuckled. "Er… Thanks, Frankie!" he said. "You really saved our lives there. Even I had started to get a bit tired of all the running!"

(Jason didn't believe that for a second.)

Frankie flushed red but didn't say anything. He just stared at the top of his staff in amazement.

I wonder if my spade can do that? Jason wondered. He looked down at the rusted spade in his hands. Somehow, it looked *worse* than before. Did it always have this strange dent in the top?

Spades are the *worst*.

Ben waved at the group. "Alright, let's go forward. *Quietly*. We don't want them coming back."

They took a step forward.

Another step.

Another.

Snap

Everyone turned to look at Jason. A twig had snapped under his foot. *Sorry,* he mouthed. Brittany shook her head.

When they finally stepped out into the glade, Jason had never felt more exposed in his entire life. Anything could jump out of the trees from anywhere, at any moment.

But for now, everything seemed safe. All they had to do was –

"What's that noise?" hissed Brittany.

They all froze and listened.

...

...

"What noise?" whispered Ben.

...

...

Mmm mmm mmm mm!

...

"Is someone humming?" asked Jason.

...

Mmm mmmm mm mmm!

...

"It sounds like a voice," said Brittany.

Mmmm mmmmm mm mm!

"Oh! It's that tree!" Brittany grinned. "The

tree is talking!" She pointed at the trunk that the gray wolf had been sniffing earlier. Ben and Jason exchanged a glance. "Hello, tree," said Brittany. "What do you want?"

MMM MMM MMMMM MM!

"The tree sounds... pretty angry," said Jason.

"And like a girl," said Ben.

"An angry girl," said Jason. His eyes widened. "You don't think –"

Ben, realizing what Jason meant, went over to the trunk of the tree, which was covered in tightly wrapped vines. He started to slice them away with his sword. Jason moved forward and began pulling leaves with his hands.

"I don't think the tree will like that," said Brittany.

Jason pulled away another clump of leaves and there, underneath all the foliage, was Ava, tied to the tree! She gasped for breath.

"Finally!" she said. "What took you so long?"

"Oh!" said Brittany. "The tree has Ava in it!"

Jason bit his lip.

Ava's eyes narrowed at him. "Don't you dare."

Jason felt tears begin to form in his eyes.

"If you laugh..." she threatened.

Pfffffff. Jason was trying to hold back.

Ben cut through another vine. "We'll have you out in a –" he began.

"HAHAHAHAHA!" Jason burst out

laughing. "You're tied to a tree! You ran off without us and got caught BY A TREE!"

Jason howled with laughter and rolled on the floor.

"Laugh all you want, *spade boy*," Ava said through gritted teeth. "When I'm cut down from here…"

Jason laughed and laughed until Brittany poked him with her foot. "Come on," she said. "Don't be rude."

"Sorry," grinned Jason, wiping away a tear. "I'll just…" He pushed himself up.

Or…at least he tried. Something was holding his arm down. He looked to the side. Vines were wrapping around him.

"Uhhhh," he said. "Guys!"

Ben was freeing Ava, and the other two were gazing into the forest – no one was looking at Jason.

More vines wrapped around his legs!

"Er… help!" he yelled.

Brittany picked something out of her large front teeth and inspected her finger.

"Help!" cried Jason.

The group turned. Ava smirked.

"Not so funny now, eh?" she said victoriously.

"Quick!" said Brittany, grabbing her brother. "Use your superpowers, Frankie!"

Frankie stepped forward and held his staff up.

Nothing happened — a vine wrapped around

Jason's head.

"Uuuuuh helff?" he said as the vines tightened around his mouth, pulling his head down into the ground.

Ben swung his sword down, cutting Jason's head free. Another swipe – *THUNK* – and his arm became free. Jason started tearing at the vines.

Brittany squeaked. A vine had wrapped around her ankle and was pulling her away! She grabbed onto Frankie.

Ben began swinging with his sword, but a vine leaped up from the ground and tightened around his blade. "Run!" he shouted at Ava. "Run while you can!"

"THERE'S NOWHERE TO RUN," a deep voice said from the side of the glade. A man with a big, red beard was standing proudly at the edge of the opening. He held a large ax in his hand, and a group of ugly and angry-looking men stood in a line behind him.

"No one escapes the glade." He grinned a black-toothed grin. "Not unless *I* want them to." He raised a hand, and the vines stopped. "Betrayna will pay a nice price for all of you!"

Ben raised his sword. "You won't get any of us! Come on, guys! Let's…"

8. NEXT LEVEL

LOADING.
PLEASE WAIT.

"…go!" shouted Ben.

Jason, mid-step, was thrown forward right into a – **THUD!** His face connected with a thick, wooden bar. Hot pain flared in his nose, and his eyes started to water.

"Owwwwww!" he said. "What is *that?* Where did that come from?"

He looked hard. It was definitely a thick wooden bar.

A second ago, there had been a forest glade in front of him. There had been vines and scary-looking men and…then the world sort of froze? He looked around. There were a lot of thick wooden bars surrounding the group. They were *locked in a cage!*

They weren't even in the forest anymore.

Jason blinked out tears as he looked around.

They were in some kind of camp. Small tents were arranged in a circle around them. The tents were made from some kind of animal skin and bones.

Small fires burned outside each of the tents. Armed men were patrolling around.

"Was that…a loading screen?" asked Ben, looking at his now empty hands. Their weapons (and Jason's spade) were all stacked in a pile near the largest of the tents.

"We must be in level two," said Ava. "I guess that's why time skipped."

"I can taste toothpaste again," said Brittany.

Jason blinked again and touched his nose. Hot pain flared across his face. He looked down at his finger. It was red with blood. He felt a bit queasy.

"Let me have a look," said Ava, irritably. Jason was suddenly aware of how close she was to his face. Their eyes met, and she paused. (Was it getting hot in this cage?) Her frown deepened, and she pulled away. "Yeah, that looks nasty. Let me just…"

She poked Jason on the nose. Pain flared again.

"Ow!" he said. "That hurt!"

"I've found the source of the problem," said Ava. "You've hurt your nose."

"I could've told you that!" snapped Jason, stepping back. Ava grinned. Jason turned to look at the others. Ben was frowning.

"What did you say?" said Ben.

Ava and Jason glanced at each other.

"*I could've told you that*?" Jason said.

"No, before that," said Ben.

"Er… *I've found the source of the problem?*" said Ava.

"No, before *that*."

Jason thought hard. "Um," he said. "Ow, that hurt?"

Ben clicked his fingers, and his frown deepened. "That! That!"

Ava tapped her foot on the floor and rolled her eyes. "Do you want us to repeat everything we have ever said, ever? Or are you actually going to explain?"

Ben didn't respond right away. He seemed to be thinking quite intensely. Jason wiggled his nose slowly. Something *clicked*. Why did these things always happen to him?

Jason slumped against the bars of the cage and winced as another flare of pain went through his face.

"You're in pain," said Ben, finally.

"Yeah," grumbled Jason. "Sorry I'm not a soccer-playing, sword-wielding mega-dude like you. Some of us don't play sports *every day of our lives* like you."

Ben shook his head. "No, I mean, that's not right. Why are you in pain?"

"Because he headbutted the cage," said Brittany, articulating clearly as though she was talking to a small child.

".. ..." said Frankie.

"Yeah, wood is hard," said Brittany. "And then Ava poked him."

"I was *examining* the damage," Ava said innocently. Jason shot her a look.

"Yes, I know, but we are *in a game*," said Ben. "We shouldn't be feeling anything."

Everyone in the cage went silent (except Frankie, since he was already silent. But his eyes widened a little).

"You know," said Ava quietly. "When I got trapped by the tree, the vines were squeezing really tight. It did hurt. I was..." she swallowed. "I was scared."

Ava stared out of the cage, turning her back to everyone.

"And I got really tired running from those wolves!" said Brittany. "My legs are still aching. What is up with that? Aren't we all still sitting in the gaming store, or whatever?"

Jason experimentally raised his arms to his head and touched his ears. He reached over to Ava and touched her ears.

"Hey!" she snapped, spinning around to face him. "What are you doing?"

"I'm trying to see if I can take off your helmet!" said Jason. He tapped her on the head, and she looked like she was about to explode. He stepped back. "I can't take off yours or mine," he quickly added.

Before Ava could say anything (or do anything violent), Ben stepped in. "This is worrying," he said. "I mean, if we can feel pain, it must mean that those helmets are linked directly into our central nervous systems and are sending messages directly to our brains. If they can do that..."

Jason looked at Brittany. She shrugged.

"If they can do that...?" Jason asked.

Ben pressed his lips together. He looked worried.

"What's it got to do with my aching legs, smart boy?" asked Brittany.

"Not smart enough to get us out of here," smiled Ben sadly.

"But wait," said Ava. "What happens if, say, Jason gets stabbed? Even if it is an *accident*." She looked at him on the last word. Jason shivered.

"I don't know," said Ben. "If we die in the game…" He took a long breath. "Just don't die, yeah?"

"Simple," grinned Jason, but inside he felt icy cold.

***

Brittany paced in the cage, occasionally glancing out to see what the men with weapons were doing outside the camp. None of them seemed to be paying attention to their prisoners. There was no way out, as far as she could see.

She chewed on her nails. Ben's words echoed in her mind. *Just don't die, yeah?* It seemed simple enough, and yet now she was looking at everything in a different light. Did she need to eat in this game? Were bacteria a thing in this game? What happened if she touched something dirty and got the flu? This cage wasn't very clean.

She stepped over Jason again. He had a big black bruise on the end of his nose, and he looked very sorry for himself. No one, in fact, seemed to be enjoying this game anymore.

The dull, dangerous game where she could feel pain and die any second.

Brittany stopped pacing. "That's it!" she said. "I can't take it anymore!" She grabbed onto the bars of the cage and began to shake them. "I need to get out of this game!"

Ben got to his feet. "Woah, woah, woah," he said. "It's okay, Brittany, it's okay!"

She turned to him; eyes filled with fury. "It's not OK!" she said. "We could die any second! Jason could get stabbed at any moment!"

"Hey!" said Jason, still holding his nose.

"Hello?" shouted Brittany. "Melissa? I'd like to leave now! Let me out please!"

Her voice echoed around the camp. A few

guards stopped to look at her. They laughed and moved on.

"Hello?!" she said again. "Test over, TEST OVER!"

Silence.

Ava and Ben exchanged a worried glance.

Brittany let out a sob. "I didn't sign up for this. Let me out. **LET ME OUT!**" She grabbed the bars of the cage again. They felt cold in her hands. She blinked away tears, but they rolled down her cheeks anyway. Brittany tried to speak again, but all that came out was a little choking sound at the back of her throat.

She tried to breathe in, but her throat was tightening. Brittany gasped, fighting for breath, and rested her head against the cage bars. She closed her eyes as her chest burned and tightened, tears hot on her cheeks.

Someone wrapped their arms around her and pulled her close. Opening her eyes, Brittany glimpsed Ava through the blur of her lashes. The smaller girl held her tight.

"Shhh," said Ava. "It's okay; we are here with you. We are scared too."

"I… It's… We…" Brittany tried to speak; each breath chopping the words too short. Finally, she broke, placing her head on Ava's shoulder and crying. Ava smelled like leather and flowers. Slowly, in Ava's embrace, Brittany felt her breath return. She calmed.

"Thank you," she croaked.

Ava smiled. "My sister gets panic attacks, too. Don't worry. We'll be fine."

Brittany smiled and wiped her cheeks. She tucked her hair behind her ear and was about to say something when –

BLOOP!

A glowing yellow square appeared in the air in front of Brittany. She stepped back from Ava as her eyes widened. "Is that…?"

Words appeared on the square.

Welcome Guardian!

CHARACTERS

SETTINGS

CREDITS

QUIT GAME

"A menu!" said Ava. "How did you open that?!" (Was that a hint of jealousy that Brittany heard in Ava's voice?)

"I… I don't know!" said Brittany. "It just opened!"

"Okay," said Ava. "What did you just do?"

"Had a panic attack," said Brittany quietly, her face hot.

"No, after that."

"Um," Brittany thought. "We hugged." Brittany pulled Ava back towards her, pushing her face into her shoulder.

"Mmff mff m!" said Ava.

"Huh?"

"I think she said *That isn't it*," said Jason.

"Oh." Brittany released Ava, who gasped for air.

"What's next?" croaked Ava.

"I pulled away, I wiped a tear," Brittany wiped her face. "No, that's not it. I tucked my hair…"

BLOOP!

The menu closed.

"My ear!" said Brittany. "I touched the back of my ear! It opens and closes the menu!"

Brittany touched her ear again.

BLOOP!

The menu opened.

She touched her ear.

BLOOP!

The menu closed.

BLOOP!

BLOOP!

BLOOP!

BLOOP!

BLOOP!

"Okay, you can stop now!" Ava said as Brittany did a little victory dance around her. "Do you want to quit the game?"

"Oh, right," grinned Brittany. She reached out and tapped the floating menu in front of her. It was like tapping on a cold window. The 'QUIT GAME' button lit up.

BWAP

Nothing happened.

BWAP
BWAP

Brittany pressed the button again and again. Her chest tightened.

"Why can't I quit the game?" she said. "The menu won't let me quit!"

"What?" said Jason. "Maybe you're doing it wrong?"

"I think I know how to press a button," grumbled Brittany, but Jason was already touching behind his ear to open the menu.

He pressed the quit button.

BWAP

The button didn't work.

Brittany cried out and dropped back to the ground.

They were trapped in the game.

9. Skill Activated

Ava was awoken by a low flying kettle. It spun through the air, over the campfire and collided with the bars of the cage with a loud…

THUMP!

She was annoyed. She had been dreaming that she was on stage with The Screaming Howlers and they were singing a song for her.

*"You're trapped in a caaaage
and that's really saaaaaad…"*

"**HAhaHa**!" A weird, bumpy sort of laugh echoed across the camp.

It was late.

Ava looked up to see the large red-headed hunter, who had caught them in the forest, making his way over to them. He had a big ugly face.

Standing in front of the cage, he bellowed out another laugh.

"**HAhAhaa**!" The laugh was really strange. It went up and down in unpredictable ways, reminding Ava of a stormy sea. "The great guardians," he grinned. "Trapped in MY cage. Betrayna will pay a large price when I deliver you!"

"Who's Betrayna?" whispered Brittany from the corner on Ava's left.

Ava groaned. "The evil sorceress," she replied. "She's the whole reason we are here!"

"Right," said Brittany. She still looked confused. Some people just didn't understand games.

"They told me it would be impossible, but here we are with all the Guardians and Player Three…" The hunter's voice took on that strange robotic tone. Ava rolled her eyes. As if Jason's head wasn't big enough. "All trapped in my cage. **HAHAhahaHa-**" the hunter paused and took in a breath. "**Haaaaaaa**!" he added.

"Did you… throw a kettle at us?" Ben asked.

The Red Hunter looked down at the floor sheepishly. "I…er… wasn't sure how to get your attention."

"So you threw a kettle?"

Ava just wanted to disappear. This was all nonsense.

"**HAAhaHAhaaa**!" laughed the hunter. "No one ever escapes from The RED HUNTER! I make sure of it because I-"

A cold feeling rushed over Ava's body. She shivered. Had someone turned down the temperature?

The Red Hunter paused and frowned. He mumbled under his breath, then said loudly: "Wait, wasn't there five of you in here before?"

Ava looked around. Ben, Jason, Brittany, Frankie - yes, everyone was still there. What was he talking about?

The Red Hunter turned around. "Hey Kevin, it was five guardians we caught, right?" He held up five fingers to a hunter who was standing by a nearby tent, picking his nose.

Kevin the hunter counted his fingers. "Yeah," he said, holding up four fingers. "We got five."

The Red Hunter looked back at the cage and counted again. "One, two, the ugly one makes three- "

"Hey," snapped Jason. "I'm not ugly!"

Ben looked towards Ava and almost jumped out of his skin. "Woah!" he said. "Where's Ava?!"

Ava frowned. Everyone was looking in her direction, but no one was *looking* at her. "I'm sitting right here," she said.

"She was sitting *right there*," said Ben, as if he hadn't heard her. "I'm sure of it."

"Hey," said the Red Hunter. "How did she get out? That's not fair! No one escapes my cages! No one! Kevin? Hernandez? Michelle? Did you see where she went?"

Three burly-looking hunters shrugged and shook their heads.

"I am right-" Ava waved her hand in front of

her and then realized she *couldn't see her hand.*

She could not see her hand. *What?* she thought. *How?*

Ava looked down at her body.

SHE WAS COMPLETELY INVISIBLE!

Okay, Okay, stay cool, she thought. *You've just discovered you're a superhero with super invisibility powers, play it cool.*

What would the Screaming Howlers do?

They would sing an awesome song about it. Since she did not have a drummer or a beautiful-eyed guitarist nearby, nor a pen and paper to write down song lyrics, she would have to figure out something else.

The Red Hunter untied the knot that held the cage door closed and pushed it open. "What is this?" he snapped. "Some kind of trick? Magic?" He stepped into the cage and shoved Jason backward.

Ava took her chance and stepped *right out* of the cage.

It took her a moment to process.

She was outside of the cage. *Outside.*

No more sitting in a cramped cage with the smell of damp mud assaulting her nostrils. No more being kicked by Jason as he tried to get comfy. She was free!

She broke into a run, dodging hunters and rushing across the camp. Ava didn't know where she was going but *away* was the general direction. She almost tripped over the pile of weapons (and one spade) at the far side of the camp. Grinning, she picked up her knives and reattached them to her armor. Now she was definitely ready to face this game!

Near the camp was a river – she had heard the rushing of water from the cage. Ava reasoned that near a river, there must be… ah ha!
A small wooden boat was tied to a tree. It bobbed gently on the water. A boat was the fastest way to escape! Ava grinned even wider and reached for the rope to undo the knot.

"I don't know!" Jason's voice squeaked in the distance. "I really don't know!"

Ava turned back. Through the gap in the tents, she could see the Red Hunter with his hand around Jason's throat.

"Well then, I'll just start chopping bits off you until someone *remembers*!" The Red Hunter snapped. "You don't need two arms, do you?"

The other hunters cheered. The rest of her group cried out. Jason screeched like a baby eagle as the Red Hunter dragged him out of the cage. Ava looked back. She could leave right now. She could complete the game. She *should* leave right now. Everyone else would slow her down.

"Wait," said Ben. "You can't do this!"

"I can do what I want!" shouted the Red Hunter. "HAhaHHHHHAAAAhahahaAHhaHA!"

Ava headed back to the camp.

10. Unlock Attempt Failed

Jason didn't realize how much he liked having two arms until there was a vicious hunter threatening to cut one off.

He was running as fast as he could around the central fire of the camp. The world was a blur around him, but he knew he had to keep running.

Somewhere, beyond his vision, people were laughing, and someone was shouting. Jason could barely hear them over the panting of his breath. He turned another corner and...

"**HAahaHA!**" The Red Hunter was standing in front of him, a wild, yellow grin beneath his red beard. "Stop moving, you maggot!" Spittle flew from his mouth, and he brought his sharp, angry-looking ax up to his face. "I wanna chop off that arm!"

"You stop moving!" squeaked Jason, his eyes wide. "It would make running away a lot easier!"

"Jason!" Ben cried out from the cage. "Look out!"

Jason ducked out of the way just before a pair of arms tried to wrap around his head. Other hunters were trying to grab him! He bolted like a desperate deer and tried to squeeze through two of the large brown tents.

WOAH!

A rope (a sneaky rope, a rope which Jason

106

was *sure* had appeared out of nowhere) held tight as it connected with Jason's ankle and he found himself hitting the grassy ground with a *flumpf*.

He rolled over, trying not to think about the burning sensation in his leg, and found the Red Hunter standing over him, blocking out the light.

"Now then," the Red Hunter said in an eerily quiet voice. "You've had your fun. It's time I had mine." He raised the ax above his head as a slow, sadistic grin darkened his face. "Are you a lefty, or a righty?"

"Eek!" squeaked Jason (later, he would realize that this wasn't the bravest thing to say before having your arm chopped off, and would tell people he had said something like, "You will never defeat me!" or *"Luke, I am your father"* or *"I am Iron Man!"*).

The firelight glimmered against the steel of the ax blade as it was raised higher. Jason winced. This was going to hurt.

"No!" A voice came out of nowhere. Ava *backflipped* over the Red Hunter's head and snatched the ax out of his hands! She landed smoothly on the other side of him, her eyes wide. Looking at the ax in her hands, she seemed as surprised as Jason felt.

She turned to him. "Run!"

Jason didn't need to be told twice.

"Hey! What? Hey!" The Red Hunter was confused, looking between Jason and Ava, unsure who to go for first. He thrust a dirty finger in Ava's direction. "Don't just stand there, you lumps!" he barked at the other hunters. "Get her!"

He set his dark eyes on Jason.

Jason had twisted back around the camp and was at the cage again, trying to undo the world's *tightest knot* with his fingers.

"Who made this knot?" The rope refused to budge.

Small letters sparkled off the top of the rope as he touched it. In cheerful, yellow letters, it said:

Unlock attempt failed!

"Come on!" he groaned.

Unlock attempt failed!

"I can *do it!*" Jason muttered to himself.

Unlock attempt failed!

"I don't think you can," Brittany sighed.

"Behind you!" Ben shouted.

Jason turned.

Standing with the campfire raging behind him, the Red Hunter looked like a demon from a dark dimension.

"I've had enough of your games," he said.

"You're not the only one," Jason replied. "I think I've had enough of games altogether."

"I'm gonna destroy you." The Red Hunter took a step forward.

"I do not feel that great today, maybe destroy me tomorrow?" Jason took a step back. The cage bars poked him. He was stuck.

"I always really liked you," Brittany said, patting Jason on the head.

"That doesn't help!" Jason growled back at her. He clenched his fist and, to his surprise, found himself holding something. He glanced at his hand. How did *that* get there?

The Red Hunter began a low, monstrous chuckle. **"HuhuhuhahAHAHAHAH!"** He broke into a run, straight at Jason, planning to crush him against the bars.

"I guess," said Jason, "I'm going to have to fight *dirty!*"

He dug his spade – which had magically appeared in his hand – into the ground and flicked upwards, spraying dust and mud right into the Red Hunter's eyes.

"Argh!" cried the Red Hunter, grasping at his face. "You *blinded* me! That's not fair!"

A dagger flew through the fire – *Thwip!* – and hit the knot holding the cage closed.

Jason looked down at it, eyes wide.

Bright pink writing sparkled out of the knot:

Unlock
Attempt
Successful!!

"Oh, come on!" said Jason.

Ava flipped over the fire and bounced off the Red Hunter's shoulders. He fell to his knees with a cry, and she landed gracefully in front of him. She looked up at Jason. "What are you doing?" she said. "Let's get out of here!"

Jason opened the cage door, and they ran. But where were they going?

11.Water Experience

Splosh

The oar sank into the murky depths of the river.

Splosh

The oar went in again. The brown water swirled.

Splosh

Yep. Still an oar. Still a river. Swirly swirl.

Splosh

Oar. Water. Swirl. (You get the idea.)

Jason stared over the edge of the boat. Their great escape had been exciting, amazing, and awesome. Jason had never experienced anything like it in his life. His heart had been pounding. He had barely escaped with his life. Everything had been on instinct. It had felt like he was inside an action game!

But now…

His legs were cramping. The boat was barely big enough to fit three of them, never mind all five.

Splosh

Ben pulled back on the oars again.

He had been rowing the boat for about two hours. He was still smiling. If he was tired, it wasn't obvious. Jason wasn't sure if this was a game power

(Unlimited Rowing? Boat Master?) or if it was just because Ben was super sporty and never got tired. Jason wished he had arms thick as tree trunks like Ben. But no, all he had was a magic spade.

"Do you do gymnastics?" Ben asked Ava.

"Nope," said Ava. "I tried tennis once, but I hit the ball so hard I broke the racket."

"No sport at all?"

"Do e-sports count?"

"Uh… I don't think so."

"Then, no."

"So, you just flipped over the guy without any training?"

Ava shrugged. "It just seemed like the right thing to do."

Ben grinned. "That's awesome."

Splosh

Nothing I do is ever awesome, thought Jason.

Jason puffed up his cheeks, holding in his mouth and then POP! He let the air go. The boat continued to float down the river.

Jason puffed up his cheeks again.

Sp-

"WILL YOU STOP THAT?" Ava suddenly shouted, whipping over toward him.

Jason blinked at her; his cheeks puffed up. He quietly let the air out of his mouth. "I would like to row the boat," Jason said.

"Huh?" said Ava.

"Yeah, I'd like to row the boat. I think Ben and I should swap."

"Really, you don't have to. It's fine," Ben said, but Jason was already standing up, the boat rocking from side to side.

"Let's switch," said Jason, stepping over Ava's leg. She rolled her eyes.

"No, really, Jason," said Ben, who had stopped rowing.

The boat wobbled a bit and began to spin. Brittany's cheeks turned green.

".. …. …" said Frankie, but Brittany was too busy covering her mouth with her hand to translate.

"Jason, stop!" said Ava. "Just sit down!

"I know what I'm doing!" said Jason. "Just give me a sec, if I can just…"

The boat thumped against something in the water.

Woah! Jason tumbled back, causing the boat to rock violently.

"Get. Off. My Lap," Ava said through gritted teeth. Jason quickly got up again.

"Listen, buddy, I got this," said Ben, picking up one of the oars. Jason snatched the other one before Ben could.

"No, no, no," said Jason. "I can-"

"You clearly can't," said Ava.

The boat shimmied and shook. Up and down. Up and down. The water was getting rough.

"Uuuuuurgh," said Brittany in a low voice.

"....?" Frankie looked at her, worried.

"Listen," said Ben, "it's fine. I'm not tired. Just give me the oar." He winced as the boat crunched against something in the water.

"You may have all the muscles in the world," said Jason, "but they get tired too, right? Let me just-"

Jason went for the other oar, and a hand grabbed his arm. He looked up to see Ava staring at him. "I'm stopping you," she said. "Before you drown us all."

"I'm not going to drown us," snapped Jason.

"Guys," said Ben. "Er…Inside boat voices?"

"Oh yeah?" said Ava. "My damp socks tell a different story!"

"Well, maybe you should just get out and swim!" said Jason.

"Just give me the oar!"

"Guys?"

"No!"

"Er, guys, seriously, you need to see this."

"UUuUuughhh,"

"Give it to me!"

"No!"

The boat rocked back and forth violently as Ava and Jason fought over the oar. The water around them was getting very white. Ava and Jason didn't notice.

"You had your chance, and you failed," snapped Ava. "Now let me have a go."

"I didn't even sit down!" said Jason. "I can get us to safety!"

"GUYS!" roared Ben. "**STOP!**"

There was silence in the boat. They all looked at Ben. But he wasn't looking at them; he was looking, eyes wide, at wherever they were going.

"We need to abandon the boat!" said Ben.

"I'm not getting in the water! No!" said Brittany.

"Why?" Jason asked. He turned to look. He turned back. "Oh. That."

He hadn't noticed it until now. The sound of crashing water somewhere nearby. The way that in the distance the water just… ended. It poured over the edge of what sounded like a very, very, *very* large waterfall.

Jason could imagine the sharp rocks at the bottom with horrifying clarity. He could also imagine the boat shattering with them inside it shortly afterward.

"Okay," said Jason. "We can get out of the boat."

Ava had a different idea. She snatched the spade from the end of the boa, and frantically started paddling. The boat just sat in the water, spinning more and more.

"Uuuuuugh…" groaned Brittany.

"Help me!" snapped Ava.

"Oh, *now* you want me to do something?" said Jason, but Ava ignored him.

They all started paddling (apart from Brittany, who was just dribbling). With spade, shield, oars, and hands, they pushed against the rushing water to try and get to the side of the river.

"We're doing it!" said Ava. "We're- "

THONK.

"What was that?" moaned Jason.

A very pale Brittany sat up, an arrow in her hand. "I found this," she said weakly.

THONK. SPLASH.

Arrows were being fired at them from the riverbank!

"**HAhaHAAA**!" came a laugh from the trees. "You cannot escape THE RED HUNTER!"

"Aww, come on," said Jason. "Really? We were so close."

Thonk! Thonk!

Two more arrows struck the side of the boat, coming from the other side of the river. They were surrounded.

"We're stuck!" said Ava. "There's nowhere to go!"

"There is one way…" said Jason.

"Oh no," said Ben. "No, No, NO!"

Jason turned to his friends in the boat as the water pulled them right to the edge.

"How bad can it be?" he grinned. Then he closed his eyes, trying to remember his swimming lessons at school.

The boat tipped over the edge, towards the roar of the water below.

12. Alternate Paths

Frankie was cold.

It was like that time Brittany had pushed him into a snow drift, only much *much* worse. Frankie hated being cold.

His arms and legs wouldn't respond. When he tried to look around, the world was blurry and white. Where was he?

Frankie opened his mouth to speak, but it immediately filled with water. He shook as his body spasmed in pain. He was choking. His lungs were on fire.

Water. He was underwater! He was in the river!

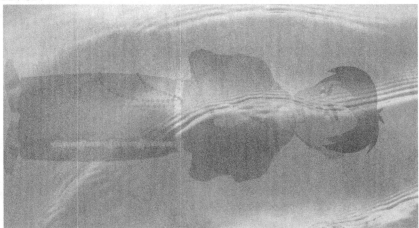

Panic kicked in, with a capital P. He was going to drown. He knew it. He was going to drown, and no one would find him, and it would be terrible and...

Stay calm, he thought. *That's what the survival*

TV shows always say. Stay calm.

With great effort, he moved one arm. Then another. He began to kick. Was he going up or down? He didn't know. The roar of blood in his ears and the rush of water was all he could hear. *Arms. Legs. Move, Frankie. MOVE!*

Panic. Panic. Darkness. Panic.

He grabbed for something, anything, as the river current carried him along. His hands found slimy rocks, handfuls of gravel. Nothing he could hold onto. He carried on floating, his lungs burning, dragged along against his will.

Panic. Panic. Panic.

Then, surprisingly, his hand wrapped around something wooden and familiar.

His staff!

As soon as he realized what it was, a pulse of warmth filled his body. The tight feeling in his chest lightened. The Panic subsided.

Being swept away down the river didn't feel like such a scary thing anymore. He felt alright. He knew he could get out of this.

Frankie kicked his legs and found himself floating steadily towards the surface. It wasn't too long before he broke through and took in a long, glorious breath of air. Light shone down on his face.

He coughed the water out and tried to get his bearings. The waterfall was quite far away - the power and the speed of the water had taken him almost around the next corner of the wide river. Mercifully, the bank was quite close. He swam, using the staff as a flotation device, and quickly found the river was shallow enough for him to stand up. Even better, there, flopped on the muddy shore, was Brittany!

But the Panic quickly returned. She wasn't moving, and her eyes were closed. He kicked and swam faster than he had ever done. He had never been on the swim team at school, but if they had seen him swim then, they would have begged him to join.

Reaching his sister, he pulled himself up next to her and checked her pulse (he had learned to do that on those survival TV programs: two fingers on the wrist or neck). He felt a weak beat of her heart. She wasn't dead! He turned her over and placed his ear near to her mouth. He listened.

There was a quiet breath. He sagged with relief.

She was just unconscious.

Frankie wasn't sure what to do. He was too small to carry her out of the water, but it was too cold to leave her here. He glanced at the staff, still clasped firmly in his hand.

It worked for him, right?

He gently pressed the crystal on top to her forehead and thought to himself: please work. Please. I'll do anything. Heal my sister.

The crystal glowed in response. It was like it was talking to him. It seemed to say: *Of course.*

The familiar warmth spread out from the staff

again and flowed through his sister. She gained color in her cheeks almost immediately. Her skin even began to glow. It was working!

A smile broke out on his face as Brittany's blue eyes snapped open and found him.

She frowned. "What are you smiling about, weirdo?"

***

Brittany wished she had a hairbrush.

Scratch that, Brittiany wished she had a hairbrush, a shower, her mango-scented shampoo, her bedroom, her straightener and that she didn't have her dumb half-brother grinning at her in a cold forest.

But all she had was a cold forest and her dumb half-brother who kept grinning at her like he had just won the lottery or something. There were some pine cones on the ground. Could a pine cone be used as a hairbrush? She reached for it but dropped it with a squeak when she realized it was covered with gross beetles.

It was cold on the riverbank. They were alone on the little muddy beach: there was no sign of Ava, Jason or Ben (how she wished *they* were here right now!). Brittany and Frankie decided to do the only thing they could think of, walking.

It was better than sitting until the hunters caught up with them. But only *slightly* better.

Brittany sighed again as she imagined her mango-scented shampoo. The way it sat in the palm of her hand, golden and smooth, the promise of clean, shiny hair...

After half an hour, she stopped. Her legs hurt, she was cold, and she didn't want to walk anymore.

Frankie turned back to her with confused eyes.

"I'm tired," she said. "I just want to sit on my bed with my laptop and watch RuPaul. Why do we have to keep going?" She slumped down on a nearby tree.

"... ...." said Frankie.

"At least we're alive?" Brittany pulled a face. "We're stuck in a freezing forest. I've covered in mud. There might be *beetles* on me. I'd say we are *barely* alive!" She folded her arms. "I've had enough of this running and being caught and falling off waterfalls and being cold, and this game is no fun at all! I want to go back to the puzzle games I play on my phone. At least you can't die in them! And my hair! Oh, my hair, how am I ever going to get these old twigs out of it? And the *beetles*, Frankie. They'll call me *beetle girl* at school! And the dirty water has messed everything up because..." she stopped.

"Why are you looking at me like that, Frankie?"

Frankie pointed at the tree she was leaning against. He opened his mouth but said nothing.

Brittany turned. From her hand, flowers and green stems were shooting out towards the tree.

She looked around her. It was like the forest was flourishing wherever she was standing, flowers opening up and growing in a beautiful array. Her eyes widened. She pulled her hand away. The flowers stopped spreading.

"What is...?" she said.

She frowned, gently putting her hand back onto the tree trunk. The flowers began to spread again, reaching higher and higher, bursting into colorful blooms. The leaves above her seemed to part, causing a warm ray of sunshine to touch her face, warming her up.

A branch reached up beside her and...

pop
pop
pop

Ripe, delicious-looking fruit appeared out of it.

Slowly, she reached up and plucked one - it looked like a strawberry- and bit into it. Her eyes widened.

"This tastes like poptarts!" she said. She threw one to Frankie. "Eat one, dweeb."

Frankie nibbled it and then shoved the whole fruit into his mouth, the juices running down his chin.

Brittany felt refreshed. She did not feel like she had just fallen down a waterfall anymore; she could even forget about the creepy pinecone beetles.

She looked down at her brother with wide eyes.

"I think…" she paused. "I think the forest likes me."

13. The Village of Mudd

"My mouth tastes like mud… and toothpaste," grimaced Jason as they pushed through the overgrown forest. He ducked under a particularly thorny-looking branch and rubbed his teeth with his finger. The taste wasn't going away.

"I think we must be in a new level," said Ben. "No way we could have survived that fall otherwise."

Jason thought back to the waterfall. He remembered the boat tipping, being thrown into the air and falling, falling towards the rocky bottom before… Then it went blank, and he had woken up on the riverbank, face-planted in the mud.

"I think I could have survived," shrugged Ava. "I would have used Jason's body to soften my landing."

"Oh, *thanks*," said Jason. Ava smiled at him, but he didn't return it.

"I'm just worried about Brittany and Frankie," said Ben, ignoring them both. He was talking *at* them, but not really paying attention. "Where could they have ended up?"

Ava placed a hand on Ben's shoulder, which Jason tried to ignore. "Hey," she said. "Don't worry. We'll find them."

Ben turned and nodded. "Yeah, you're right. They can't be too far away. We've just got to keep looking and then… uh…"

Jason nearly walked into Ava's back as the group suddenly stopped. Jason frowned. "What's going on?"

He bounced up to look over the tall form of Ben and then he saw it: the tight, overgrown mass of twigs, trees, branches and bushes peeled away into flat fields with roads and fences. They had reached the edge of the forest!

"Is that a village?" said Ava. "Have we found civilization?!"

Ben sighed in relief. "Phew," he said. "Maybe we can find someone here that'll help us find Brittany and Frankie!"

Jason's stomach rumbled. "And maybe get something to eat?" he asked.

The road to the village was less of a road and more of a thick line of heavy, wet mud. Their feet sank in with every step, their shoes disappearing beneath the deep brown mass.

Squelch went their feet. *Squelch. Squelch. Squirt. Splat.*

Every. Step. Took. Forever.

When they finally reached the edge of the village, a small sign hung from a post jammed into the ground.

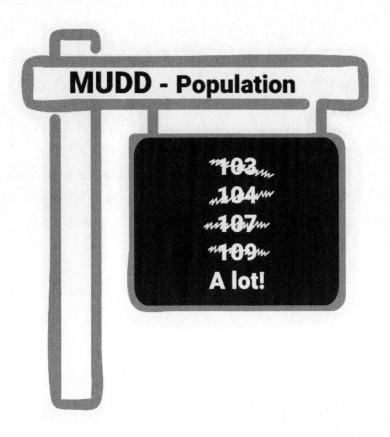

MUDD - Population

103
104
107
109
A lot!

Ben flicked some mud off his once-shiny armor. "Well," he chuckled, "at least the name is appropriate!"

Jason's stomach rumbled again. "Do you think we can find some food here?"

Ava rolled her eyes. "Maybe mud pie?"

"I'm sure we'll find something…" Ben grinned. "Unless we get in a MUDdle!"

Jason snorted.

"What was that?" said Ava, a look of concern on her face. "Was that a pun?" she said. "Don't do that."

"You never know," said Jason. "We might be able to dig up some DIRT on Betrayna here!"

Ben chuckled and punched Jason playfully on the arm.

"Puns give me a migraine." Ava shook her head. "I can feel one coming on now."

"I'm sorry, Ava," said Ben. "I wouldn't want to SOIL our relationship!"

Jason and Ben were laughing now.

"I don't need either of you or your puns!" shouted Ava, and she stormed off into the village.

The village wasn't much to look at. A few old wooden buildings grouped together, leading to a central square. The buildings looked like they could fall down at any minute. Some had doors hanging off, holes in their roofs and walls. It didn't seem like a very nice place to live.

The people of the village were dressed in muddy rags. Their faces seemed constantly glum or frowning, and if you accidentally made eye contact with one (and it would be an accident because they tried to avoid it at all costs) the villagers would turn around and quickly move in the opposite direction.

The only people who didn't seem to be in such a sorry state were the guards. Wearing bright, shining armor, they stalked around the village with cruel grins on their faces, kicking mud at the inhabitants and laughing at them.

Even Ava stopped at the sight of them, letting Ben and Jason catch up.

The three walked closer together, trying not to

draw attention to themselves.

"I don't think we should stay here long," whispered Ben.

"I agree," said Jason.

"Those guards are *definitely* bad guys," Ava added. "They aren't even *trying* to be nice."

Ben grabbed them both by the sleeve. "In here," he said. "Quickly."

He dragged them both into a wooden building that was bigger than most.

It was dark - really dark - apart from a few candles dotted here and there on tables. Around those tables sat grumpy villagers who looked up at the group as they entered.

For once, it was Jason, in his damp, muddy clothes, who felt like he fit in the most. He waved limply at them, and slowly everyone returned to their food, a few villagers shaking their heads.

At the far end of the room, a big bearded man stood behind a bar. He held a wooden tankard and was staring at us.

He sniffed loudly and spat into the tankard.

"Are we allowed in here?" Jason asked. "None of us are twenty-one." His stomach rumbled again as he looked at the food on the tables.

"Let's just grab some food, and get out of here," said Ben. "I'll sort this out."

They went up to the bar and Ben leaned on it, trying to blend in with the villagers who were doing something similar. In his shining armor, he stuck out like a pig on a chicken farm.

"Um," said Ben, clearing his throat and trying to speak in a deeper voice. "Can we have some bread?"

"Eh?" said the barman. Closer up, Jason could make out that even though he was bald on top, he had a pretty serious monobrow.

"Bread," said Ava louder. "We are hungry. We want food."

"Ah," said the barman and then he froze in place, his eyes glazing over.

"Um," said Jason. "Is that normal?"

Ava shrugged. "I've never been in a bar before."

A green menu appeared in the air next to the barman. It hovered there unnaturally, but none of the villagers seemed to react to it.

"Make your choice. I have plenty of options!" the barman said in a weird robotic voice.

Jason looked at the menu:

```
BREAD: 1 GOLD
WATER: 1 GOLD
STEAK: 5 GOLD
WINE: 5 GOLD
```

"Um," said Ben. "We don't have any gold, though."

"Make your choice. I have plenty of options!" the barman repeated.

"I don't think he can hear you," said Ava.

"Make your choice. I have plenty of options!" the barman said.

"Wow, that's annoying," Ava whispered.

"Make your choice. I have plenty -!" Ava poked the 'bread' option on the menu with her finger. The word went red.

"No gold, no service." The barman was suddenly animated again; the menu disappeared, and he waved them away.

Jason sighed. His stomach rumbled loudly as he turned away.

"I guess we should keep going," said Ben.

"Yeah," said Jason. "Maybe we will find some gold before the next village. I really wanted that bread."

"What do you think we should do now, Ava?" said Ben. They both turned. "Ava?"

Ava had disappeared.

"Not again," groaned Jason.

***

Ava had never stolen anything before.

Well, unless you counted her sister's clothes, but she always returned them.

Or the occasional cookie from the jar her mom kept on top of the refrigerator.

Or that one time she needed to pass a test and the answers were right there on the teacher's desk…

Ava had never stolen anything *serious* before.

Right now, she was hungry, she could turn invisible, and they needed to move on quickly. It seemed like the perfect time to try out her thieving skills.

She prepared a mental to-do list:

1. Find a person with money
2. Take money from the person with money
3. Eat breakfast.

Seemed simple enough. She smiled to herself as she darted out of the Unicorn's Nostril. Getting away from the boys had been easy. They *never* paid attention.

Turning invisible was easier than the first time. All she had to do was wish herself away, and it seemed to work. A cold feeling spread across her body, like stepping into a cold shower, and she felt herself melt into the shadows.

A shout from across the muddy square caught her attention. There was a small market set up, with a few sellers shouting at anyone who dared to get close enough. The closest stall had a thin, grubby-looking man behind it. On the table in front of him were chickens held in cages which were far too small for them. He waved frantically at anyone within a few meters' reach.

Her first thought was: Oh, poor chickens.

Her second thought was: Hey, he probably has money!

Her third thought was: I hope no one can hear the rumbling of my stomach…

She squelched through the mud, crossing the village square. The thin man raised his arms again as she got closer, causing her to duck quickly, so he didn't hit her in the face.

"ALL THE CHICKENS YOU COULD POSSIBLY... CHICKEN FOR!" he squeaked in a high-pitched voice. As people darted away, he puzzled to himself: "Chicken for? That didn't make sense, did it..."

The smell of unhappy chicken was thick in the air around the stall. Ava had to hold her breath; it was so rotten. How could anyone buy anything from here?

Then she saw it. A small brown purse attached to the belt of the man. It jingled with coins every time he moved.

Bingo!

She crouched down and inched towards the purse. Her heart began to thump. Her fingers wrapped around the tie that held it to the belt. Slowly, she began to undo the knot-

"Bawk. Buk. Buk," one of the chickens said. She glanced over. The chicken was squashed in the cage, with no room to move around. It made a very sad chicken sound. Ava tried to ignore it.

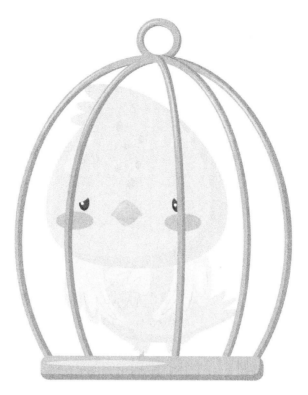

"Buk, buk." If Ava had spoken chicken, she would have heard: *Oh, woe is me, I am but a poor chicken and life has dealt me the cruelest of hands. I am doomed. Doomed!*

The knot untied, and the purse fell into her hands with a soft clink. She had done it! Now all she had to do was get back to the Unicorns' Nostril.

"Buk bawk." Ava swore the chicken was looking directly at her. She shook it off. She didn't have time for this.

"Baaaaaaawk," the chicken said. Ava was certain that she saw a tiny chicken tear roll down its chicken-y cheek.

No, she thought. *I just need to return with the*

money and then we can-

"Baw baw bawwwwwk," the chicken said. Was the chicken judging her? Ava bit back a scream of frustration. Why did this happen to her? Why couldn't she just walk away? They weren't even real chickens!

Fine, thought Ava. *No one can see me anyway.* With a gentle flick of her fingers, the lock of the chicken cage came loose.

BAWWWWWWWWWWWWWK!

Chickens BURST out of the cage in a stream of feathers, squawks and frantic flapping. The thin man behind the stall shrieked and fell backward.

Ava was sure of two things:

1. Those chickens *really* wanted to be out of that cage.

2. She definitely wasn't invisible anymore.

The man looked at her, wide-eyed. His eyes fell to the purse that was in her hands.

"Er," said Ava. "You dropped this?"

"Thief!" he screeched at the top of his lungs. "Guards! We have a thief!"

14. Combat Encounter!

"… and that's the offside rule in soccer," Ben said. "Now, there was one match-"

Jason struggled to keep his eyes open. Was all sport this boring in real life? It didn't seem that boring when he played it as a video game. His eyelids felt heavy. Maybe he could take a nap right here in the tavern. Would anyone notice?

"-The referee disagreed with the goalkeeper, and it was *crazy*. They were shouting and…" Ben suddenly paused and looked towards the door. He frowned. "Uh… Jason?"

"Hmm? Huh? What? Soccer?" Jason sat back up. A coaster unstuck itself from his forehead and flopped back onto the table.

Ben was standing up. "Ava's in trouble!" he yelled.

"How do you-" Jason didn't get to finish his sentence because Ben was already running out of the door. "Wait! Ben!" Jason picked up his spade and chased after him.

As he pushed open the tavern door, his eyes widened. Ava sprinted past on the muddy streets in front of him.

"Sorrysorrysorrysorry!" she said, pushing people out of the way and bouncing through the mud as quickly as she could.

"Catch the thief!" bellowed the two heavily

armed guards chasing after her. "For Betrayna!"

"Oh, that's not good," said Jason. "What should we do, Ben?" He turned. He was talking to himself. Ben had already started chasing after the guards!

"I really hoped you wouldn't do that," mumbled Jason and, once again, he started to run.

***

Ava was cornered. She wasn't sure how it had happened, but in her blind panic to get away, she had run down an alleyway between two buildings. There was no exit here. Just a high, wooden wall. She looked up at it desperately. Perhaps she could do some cool acrobatics like she had at the camp?

She ran at the wall and *jumped…*

…

…

Thump!

She hit the wall. Hard. She tumbled back onto the floor.

"Ugh," she groaned, wet mud seeping into her leggings. "This must be what it feels like to be Jason."

A long shadow formed on the wall in front of her. Ava turned to see a very large, angry-looking guard blocking the way out. He had a sharp sword drawn.

"Your time is at an end, *thief*," he rumbled in a deep voice.

"Um, I don't suppose you take bribes?" Ava nervously joked. She patted the pockets of her black armor, but they were all empty. She had lost the gold! All of this was for nothing! "Oh, great," she groaned.

"The only bribe I'll take is your *head*," snarled the guard. He stepped into the dark alley.

Ava took a deep breath. She drew her knives. Her hands were shaking. "D-d-don't come any closer," she said. "I'm w-warning you!"

Clang! She dropped the smaller knife.

The guard laughed cruelly at her. She felt her

face flush red.

Come on, Ava! She thought. *You can do this! You're good at games!*

She prepared to fight.

***

In most of the games Jason had played, chases were awesome. Sprinting through danger, leaping through and over obstacles, completing challenges, racing as fast as you could against the clock: they always got Jason's heart pumping, and he loved it.

This chase, however, was nothing like that. He slipped on mud. It oozed all over his feet. He seemed to run at the pace of a snail on a Sunday stroll. Everyone ran much faster than he did and quickly disappeared into the distance. Would Jason ever be able to catch up to them?

Yes. He *had* to. Jason gripped his spade tighter and gritted his teeth. He could *do* this.

Splat splat splat. He sped up. He was going to catch up. He was- *woah- WOAH!*

SQUELCH!

He fell right on his face. Mud squished into his mouth and coated his hair.

Jason lay on the floor and looked into the distance.

Being the chosen one was *the worst*.

Just in front of him, a small, brown purse rested on the ground. Jason reached out and picked it up.

***

Ava stared at the chaos, frozen to the spot. The guard had been advancing on her, ready to cut her down, when Ben had charged out of nowhere, roaring like a lion!

He had caught the guard in a footballer's tackle, pushing him to the ground.

Ava had managed to use the distraction to slip out of the alley, but now Ben was fighting the giant guard with his sword and shield!

The monster of a guard brought his sword down onto Ben . *CLANG!* Ben caught the sword with his shield, swinging his own sword in a low arc. The guard jumped back but quickly regrouped, pressing forward for another attack.

Ava didn't know what to do. She knew she should help but… how?

More guards appeared in the distance, drawing their swords.

Ben parried another attack, barely stopping the giant's sword this time. He looked tired.

"Run, Ava!" he barked out, kicking back one of the guards, causing him to stumble. "Run!"

"But-"

CLANG!

"RUN!"

Ben charged past the guard, knocking him over like a bowling pin. He ran down the street towards the other approaching guards, bellowing a battle cry and holding his sword above his head.

Ava knew what she was supposed to do, but she didn't like it. She turned away from the fighting.

She ran.

15. Skill Trees

Frankie tapped his staff against a tree. He wiggled it in the air. He tried blowing on it. He tried saying every magic word that he knew.

Abracadabra.
Shazam.
Nothing.

**The staff was no better than
your everyday walking stick!**

"You're a weirdo; you know that?" Brittany said as they continued to walk through the forest. Everywhere she put her foot, the ground grew greener, and small flowers sprouted. It was a lot less scary in the forest now that it liked her. It took care of everything they needed - food and shelter.

Frankie gave up on his staff with a quiet sigh. He tugged on his ear to make the menu open.

Bloop!

A bright yellow square appeared in the air in front of him. Words materialized onto it.

"The quit button still doesn't work," said Brittany. "Believe me, I tried."

Frankie ignored her. He looked at the menu.

"Hey," said Brittany. "Are you listening? I said I tried." She poked him in the shoulder. He brushed off the leaf that sprouted from his robe. "Ugh, you're so annoying," Brittany groaned.

Frankie stared at the menu; his head tilted slightly to the side. Was there something else they could do with it?

Frankie selected the CHARACTERS option on the menu.

Bloop!

A whole new screen opened up.

"Woah," said Brittany. They both stared at the screen, which said:

-Guardians-

PLAYER ONE –

The SHADOW THIEF
Skills:
Acrobatics
Invisibility

PLAYER TWO –

The BRAVE KNIGHT

Skills:
12!73*uehUdk#*2e
###£84urhffy####

PLAYER THREE –

The CHOSEN ONE

Skills:
Spade
Choice

PLAYER FOUR –

The DRUID of NATURE

Skills:
Commune with Nature
Animal Kindness

PLAYER FIVE –

The HOLY CLERIC

Skills:
Guidance
Protection

"Huh," said Brittany. "Well, that's a lot of words."

Frankie nodded. This was why Ava could turn invisible, and Frankie could heal and shoot light beams - it was the skills of their characters! Now, if only Frankie knew how to access those skills...

They both looked closer at the screen.

"Huh," said Brittany. "What's up with the Knight's skills? They look all messed up."

Frankie shrugged. He really didn't understand this game.

"I guess that's Ben," she said, clicking her tongue against the roof of her mouth. "What kind of skill is *spade*?"

"... ...." Frankie said.

"Use your guidance skill to find the others?" Brittany shrugged. "I guess. If you can get that staff to work."

Frankie tugged on his ear again. The menu closed.

He held his staff in the air and closed his eyes. He tried to focus on guidance. Guidance. *GUIDANCE*. Guidey guidey guidance of guidanceness.

Nothing happened.

Brittany snorted. "I guess not. You're a real help, as usual." She started walking away.

Frankie lowered his staff and looked at it. What was he doing wrong? It had worked so well before.

Brittany made a flower grow next to her. The green stem curled around her wrist, and a beautiful yellow flower popped open. She admired her new bracelet and waved it in Frankie's face. "I guess some of us are just better at this kind of thing than others. I have *no problem* using my powers."

Frankie felt a lump in his throat. He tried to swallow, but it wouldn't go away. Why was it always like this? No matter how much he tried, he just couldn't get it right. Brittany was always better than him. She could talk to anyone; she was confident; she was a leader. Frankie was always the smaller brother – *half*-brother, as Brittany liked to point out – and anything that went wrong was his fault. Maybe it was something that Brittany had from her side of the family. Something that Frankie would never have. He just wasn't good enough.

Brittany raised an eyebrow. "Aw, are you crying? Don't be such a cry-baby, Frankie."

Frankie's eyes stung, and he blinked to get rid of the tears that were forming. Why couldn't he be brave, like Brittany?

"Ugh, you're making this whole thing uncomfortable," groaned Brittany.

He wished the rest of the group were here. Brittany didn't make him feel so bad when they were around.

The staff began to glow.

We shall find them. A warm voice echoed in his mind. *They are not all lost.* He looked up at Brittany. She stared at him.

For the briefest of seconds, he caught a look in her eye - was she... scared?

She quickly turned away. "Alright, I guess you aren't so useless after all," she said. "Do you know where to go?"

ThOOOOM!

A light beamed out from the end of his staff, like a powerful lighthouse shining over a dark sea. It shot out in a straight line through the forest ahead of them.

"Well," said Brittany, "that's handier than Google Maps!"

She began walking and didn't look back.

Quietly, Frankie followed.

16. Harder Difficulty

Ben was gone.

Ben was gone.

No matter how much he kept saying it to himself, the thought just didn't want to sit in his head. It bounced around like an echo in a deep cavern.

Ben was *gone*.

How was he gone? They had searched around Mudd, but it was like he never existed. No one remembered seeing their brave friend, sprinting at full speed in shining armor through the muddy streets. No one remembered him fighting the city guards. The bartender just shrugged when Jason begged him for help. No one knew where Ben was.

Or they didn't want to tell them.

Jason and Ava were alone.

Jason hadn't realized how much he would miss Ben's chuckles, or his voice of reason, until it was gone. When they eventually decided to move on, neither he nor Ava seemed to know where they were going. They just *walked*. The muddy path wound its way through the hills, growing rockier and harder as it approached the mountains in the distance. The sun began to set, casting an orange glow across the land which slowly turned into a soft, painful red.

They walked.

They were silent.

After walking for what felt like a lifetime, Ava stopped. The rocky path split into two directions. Dark and scary, or scary and dark. Neither seemed like a good option. It was getting harder to see, so Jason patted down his legs, searching for his phone to use as a torch.

Oh yeah, Jason remembered. All he had was a muddy, smelly spade.

Ava looked left and right. She looked left again. Then, she looked right.

She took a step forward, near a large rock at the side of the road and sat down. She rested her chin on her knees and stared off into the distance.

"Um…" said Jason. "Are we stopping?"

Ava didn't respond. She just kept staring.

"Okay," said Jason. He sat down next to her. "My feet were hurting anyway."

They were both silent for a very long time.

It wasn't because they didn't have anything to say. Jason, in fact, had *many* things to say. He wanted to ask which way they were going, how they were going to survive without Ben, how they were going to survive without *food,* how they were going to do anything at all, now that it was just the two of them. But he couldn't find the words. Nothing seemed right. So, he sat, and he stared, just like Ava.

"It doesn't make sense," Ava suddenly said, breaking the silence.

Jason blinked. "Uhhh-"

Ava turned to him. "I mean, I'm good at games." Even in the twilight, Jason could make out that her face was red and blotchy. Had she been crying?

"I am really good at games," she said. "I was even thinking about getting into e-sports in the future. I am *that* good. I just needed a team…" her voice cracked. "I don't get it. How can I be so bad at this game? Games are my… well… they are everything to me." She frowned and stared at the floor. "Ben is gone. We don't even know what is happening to him right now."

"I think-" Jason began.

"What if he is being hurt, Jason?!" she asked. "It's all my fault!"

"Well-"

"What if he is dead?" Ava squeaked.

"If-"

"Or worse?" Her eyes were wide.

Jason thought about it. "What's worse than being dead?" he asked.

Ava blinked at him. Had he said the wrong thing?

"You-" she paused. "You're stupid."

She then made a little noise - a little choking sound - and he thought she was crying again. He tried to shuffle closer.

"Ava, I-." He frowned. "Are you laughing?"

"This is so stupid!" she laughed. "I feel so

stupid, and I am stuck with you - and you're stupid!" She fell back laughing, a full, raucous belly laugh.

Jason found himself laughing too. They laughed so much; they rolled on the floor until their stomachs hurt and they both lay there, looking up at the stars.

Jason took a long breath. "Listen, Ava, sometimes people go away, and it's hard. You can't know what they are doing or what they are thinking - sometimes you don't even know why they've gone. But you've just got to keep pushing on. It's not easy, but, well…" Jason propped himself up on his elbow. "I think it's what Ben wanted. For us to finish this, right?"

Ava looked up at him, her eyes big and dark in the dim light. "You've lost someone before? Outside of the game?"

Jason shrugged. "My mom isn't around." He looked at the horizon, watching the sun finally sink out of view. "I don't know where she is." He felt his throat tighten. "Anyway," he said, words pouring out of him now. "You're really brave and stuff. I don't think I would have gone off on my own into a forest, or saved us back at the cage, or tried to get the gold in the village. You are really good at games, Ava, but it just didn't go our way this time."

"But what about Ben?" Ava said, no longer looking at him.

"We'll find Ben, I know I," Jason said. He felt confident about what he was saying, but he wasn't sure why. He didn't know where it was coming from, but there was a warmth inside him that told him that everything was going to be okay. "In fact, I was playing KNIGHTS OF ZEMBALORE once, and there was a quest a lot like this one. You are trapped in a cave and-"

Ava's hand smacked Jason's arm.

"Ow! What was that for?"

"You play KOZ?!" she said, her eyes wide. "That's my favorite game!"

Jason's eyes widened. "It's my favorite game too!"

Ava sat up. "Tell me what level you are! Have you fought the dragon? Do you know about the level boost in Farout Cave?"

Jason felt a grin spread across his face. He knew about all of that. He opened his mouth to speak when Ava clasped her hand over it and looked back down the path. "What is that?" she said.

A beam of light, a kind of torch but more focused and slower, was whizzing towards them.

Jason stood up. "What do you think?" he said. "Dangerous?"

"Oh, yeah," said Ava. "Run?"

"Run!" Jason agreed.

They both started running down the dark and scary path.

But they weren't going fast enough. The path in front of them was barely visible, and they kept stumbling on stray rocks that stuck out of the ground. Every time they stopped to pick each other up, the light got closer. The gap between them and whatever creature was out to get them was lessening.

"We need to go faster!" shouted Ava. The light was so close now.

"It's not working!" cried Jason. "We're too slow!"

"What shall we-"

Ava didn't get to finish her sentence. Jason, without thinking, stepped between Ava and the oncoming light.

The fear was too great, and he closed his eyes, waiting for the impact.

He waited.

He waited a bit more.

He opened one eye.

The light had stopped in the air, right in front of him.

It just… hovered, right at the tip of his nose.

Ava looked between him and the light. She punched Jason in the arm.

"Ow!" said Jason. "What was that for?"

"You are the chosen one, stupid!" she snapped. "I need to protect you! You can't go throwing yourself between danger and me." She took a breath. "I need you to finish the game!"

Jason blinked at her. He looked at the light. He looked at her. "Sorry?" he said. He looked down. At some point during the run, Ava had grabbed his hand. Or had he grabbed hers? He couldn't remember. They looked at each other. Something softened in her face.

"Are we interrupting something? Frankie and I can come back later." Brittany's voice made them both jump and turn.

Brittany and Frankie were standing further down the path, back the way they had come. The beam of light slowly retreated back into Frankie's staff. Frankie leaned on it and grinned.

"It was you?" Ava said, snatching back her hand. She walked towards them, anger on her face. "The light that chased us was *you*?"

Brittany took a step back, worried. "Well… it was mostly Frankie."

Ava stomped up to them. Jason was worried that she was going to yell, but instead, she wrapped her arms around them.

"You're okay," she choked. "You're both

okay."

Brittany and Frankie wrapped an arm around her too.

"Yeah," said Brittany. "We're okay."

"… …?" said Frankie.

"You're right," said Brittany. "Where's Ben?"

Ava burst into tears.

17. Secret Unlocked!

"Why are mountains *so high?*" complained Brittany.

"And are they always this spooky?" added Jason.

Ava, for once, agreed with Jason. These mountains *were* creepy. After a painful night of trying (and failing) to sleep on rocks, they had woken to heavy air, thick with a damp fog that concealed everything around them. Beyond a few meters, they were surrounded by a white sheet of nothing. All they could hear was the soft crunch of their footsteps and the occasional wail of something far in the distance.

The something wailed again. It was a high-pitched roar - almost like a scream.

The group stopped and looked around.

"H-how much further F-Frankie?" asked Brittany, her voice barely above a whisper.

"… …. …" said Frankie.

"What did he say?" asked Ava.

Brittany grimaced. "He doesn't know. He just knows that we are going the right way."

Ava looked at the white fog in front of them. "But how does he know?" she whispered.

Another roar scream. From behind them this time. It seemed to be answering the first one.

"Nevermind," said Ava. "Let's just keep moving."

The group started moving quicker. Ava noticed that they were all standing a lot closer together. Frankie, at the front, was the only one who seemed to walk confidently. Jason pulled his spade closer to his chest. Ava gripped the hilts of her daggers. She could hear her breath loudly in her ears. The fog made her feel like they were trapped in a box and surrounded by *whatever* it was that was out there.

A third roar scream. This one was long and almost sad. It was also loud. Whatever it was, it was getting closer.

Brittany squeaked and bounced away from the sound. The group stopped. Ava noticed that whenever her feet touched the ground, there was a puff of green grass that sprouted out of the ground.

"That was too close," whispered Jason. "We need to get away from here."

"Should we turn around?" asked Ava, drawing her daggers now.

"I think-"

"Hey!" said Brittany loudly. "Stop!"

She ran off into the fog.

"Brittany!" Ava's eyes widened. She looked around. Frankie was gone too! She looked at Jason. "Frankie must have kept walking when the rest of us stopped!"

"And now Brittany's run off too!" Jason moaned. "I *really* don't want to go into the fog."

"Okay, okay, okay," Ava said. "We can do this." She looked at Jason. "Right? We can do this?"

Jason clutched his spade close and nodded, his face pale under his messy hair. Ava didn't feel very confident.

"Okay." She held her daggers in front of her, and they both slowly walked forward into the fog.

In the distance ahead of them, the something screamed.

***

Frankie couldn't see where he was going, but he *knew* where he was going. It was a very odd sensation. His staff seemed to pull him in a certain direction, and now it was guiding him away from the path and into the fog.

He stepped carefully from rock to rock, the ground getting wetter and more bog-like around him. If he wasn't careful, he could get stuck in the mud.

"Hey, Frankie," Brittany said from behind him, jumping between rocks. "Hey, stupid, stop! It's, not, safe!"

Frankie slowed, not because Brittany told him to, but because he came to the edge of a deep gorge. The ground fell away in front of him, a sharp cliff edge. The fog was thick and swirling beneath him, so he couldn't tell how deep it went. Something told him it was a long way down. A *very* long way down.

SPLOSH.

"Oh, come on!" Jason groaned from behind.

"I *told* you not to step in the mud!" Ava's voice echoed around him. "It's a bog!"

"It didn't look that wet," whined Jason. "How was I supposed to know?"

"Because I told you!" Ava snarled.

Frankie was aware that Brittany had caught up with him. She was standing next to him, looking into the gorge.

"I think your power is broken, Frankie," she said. "You've gotten us lost."

Frankie looked at his sister. She crossed her arms and frowned at him. "Can we go back to the path now?" she asked.

He was about to turn back to the path, just

like Brittany wanted. Frankie didn't want to argue or to make her upset. But the staff pulled him a different way. *Go forward;* it seemed to say, right off the edge of the cliff.

"Uhhh… Frankie?" said Jason. "You okay?"

Frankie blinked. He looked down into the gorge in front of him and turned back to them.

There was another scream in the distance. Then another. Then a third. Quick. Loud. Close.

"That's quite a drop, buddy," said Jason. "Maybe you should come back."

"Yeah," said Ava. "We need to go."

"Frankie!" snapped Brittany. "Stop being such a weirdo! We need to GO!" She grabbed his arm and pulled. But he wouldn't move.

Another scream. Something splashed in the bog.

"Frankie," said Jason. "Frankie!

But Frankie wasn't listening. He looked down at his staff. It hadn't caused him any trouble yet. It had just been helpful. He could trust it.

Brittany hit him on the arm. "Frankie, stop it!"

Frankie stepped forward over the edge of the cliff.

"NO!" someone screamed, but he wasn't sure who it was.

***

Instead of falling, Frankie's foot found a soft area. It like stepping on freshly trimmed grass.

172

The world around him, wobbled and faded. There was a bright light, and a voice boomed in his head:

SECRET AREA DISCOVERED

As the world re-materialized, he realized he was standing in a cave. The air around him was warm and smelled like toothpaste. He felt safe.

Brittany stumbled into the cave after him.

She blinked and looked around. "It's… what… how…" She couldn't form words. Frankie found himself grinning.

The group followed him slowly, each stepping off the edge in turn, and finding themselves in a big cave, lit up by lanterns, with green moss coating the walls.

Frankie blinked. Around them, in the moss, was food. Glorious food. Chocolate bars. Candy.

Sandwiches. Cans of soda. Every snack they could have wanted was available to them.

Jason burst out laughing and started gathering everything up.

"Woah…" said Ava. "A secret area like… like…"

"Like Farout Cave in *KOZ*!" Jason finished her sentence. They both laughed and hopped around, picking up candy and shoving it in their mouths.

Frankie didn't know what they were talking about, but he was glad they were happy.

They all sat down and rested, eating food. Frankie realized that the longer they spent in the cave, the less tired they felt. Very soon, Frankie felt like he had slept for a full night on a comfy bed.

"Guys!" Brittany cried out as she looked around the cave. "Look at this!"

She picked up a brown piece of paper and unfolded it. It was big. She lay it out on the cave floor, and they gathered around it to look.

There were marks all over the paper. One that looked like trees, another which looked like a campsite, a river, a village, a mountain…

"It's a map!" said Ava. "It's a map of where we've been!"

Jason got down on his hands and knees following the trail with his finger, all the way to a dark, twisted looking castle at the end. "Then this must be…"

"… …" said Frankie. He nodded.

"The city of Completia," repeated Brittany. "That's where Bethany is."

"*Betrayna,*" Ava said.

Brittany nodded. "Yeah, yeah, her."

"We are so close," Jason said quietly. "I didn't realize."

175

"… ….." said Frankie, quieter than ever. He had known, but no one listened to him.

"I think... we can *do this*," said Brittany. "I think we will actually be able to get out of the game. If we can-"

SCREEEEEEEEEEEEEEEEEEEEEEEE!

A loud scream-roar bounced off the walls of the cave. Everyone spun towards the entrance of the cave, weapons drawn.

"We're safe in here, right?" said Jason.

No one replied.

"Right?" he squeaked.

THUMP

THUMP

THUMP.

Something big entered the cave.

The group looked up, and up, and up.

Brittany screamed.

18. Fast Travel

It was a pig. A giant, hairy pig. Its snout was about the same size as Jason's head, and the *smell…* Oh, wow, the smell.

The pig took up the entire entrance to the cave and stared at them all with big, golden eyes. This wasn't your normal pig! It didn't take them long to work out that it was this pig that had been making all the noise in the fog.

It took even less time for Brittany to leap forward and wrap herself around the leg of the pig, hugging it tightly.

"It's *so cute!* she said, petals floating down around her. "I want to keep it forever!"

Ava and Jason looked at Frankie. He shrugged.

"Uh… At least it isn't trying to eat us?" Jason tried, but the whole situation felt weird. He tried not to pull a face as Brittany started kissing the pig on its chin. The pig let out a loud, happy *oink* and trembled in response. It seemed to like her as much as she liked it.

"Awww, you're a sweet wiggly piggy, aren't you?" Brittany said, reaching up to scratch its cheek. It snorted in response and wiggled its nose.

"Much as I would love for us to all stand here and admire the giant pig monster," Ava said, "We kind of need to get going? You know, Betrayna and Completia? All that? Escaping the game?"

Brittany's eyes lit up. "I know how we are going to get to the capital!" she grinned, turning to look at the group.

Jason looked between her and the pig. It clicked in his head what she wanted to do. "Oh no," he said. "Oh no, no no no-"

***

To be fair, they did manage to get off the mountains in less time than if they had been walking (at least, so said Brittany and Ava. Jason still had doubts). Sitting on the back of the pig, pressed between Frankie and Ava, was not the most comfortable experience of his life.

He lost feeling in his legs after about ten minutes and shuffled uncomfortably. He still wasn't sure that the pig wouldn't try to eat them and that this wasn't all just an elaborate ruse on its part. Maybe the pig was just taking them to a huge pig camp where they would be trapped in *another* cage, waiting to be roasted on a stick.

No, Jason *did not trust* this pig.

It rocked him again as if it knew what he was thinking. *Ugh.* Maybe he shouldn't have eaten so much treasure candy back in the cave.

"Are you okay, Jason?" Ava's voice came from behind him.

Jason nodded. It was best not to speak, just in case all the 'treasure' came back up.

The pig plodded onwards, each stride taking them further along the mountain path. Quite quickly, the fog peeled away, and the group could see into the distance. Ahead of them, the world opened up into a large valley, with steep mountains on either side. At the other end of the valley, surrounded by a wide river and a deep, sprawling forest, was a great city. The tops of towers and spires poked out above the walls that ran all the way around. Built in a smooth white stone, the city shone in the sunlight as if it were made from silver. It would have been a perfect fairy tale picture, if not for the large plumes of black smoke that billowed up in the sky, corrupting the clear air.

"Well," said Ava. "That was unexpected."

Brittany brought the pig to a stop. She scratched it behind the ears and whispered to it as the rest of them stared at the city.

"Okay," said Jason. "I guess we need a plan. I doubt we could just walk right in."

"Why not?" said Brittany.

"Betrayna."

"Who?"

"The bad guy!" snapped Ava.

"Oh."

"Why don't we just smash down the front gates with the giant pig?" said Ava. "Figure out the rest from there?"

"Her name is Snuffles," said Brittany. "And I don't want her hurting her little nose!" she said, stroking the top of Snuffle's head. The pig wiggled her ears happily in response.

"Well," said Ava. "I could turn invisible and… er…"

"Then we would lose you again," said Jason. "No, let's stick together."

".. …. …" suggested Frankie.

"Yes!" said Brittany. "Disguises! I LOVE dressing up!"

"We could all sneak in unnoticed!" Jason grinned.

"Oooh, like in *KOZ* in the City of Thieves expansion?" Ava said.

"Exactly! You can get your knight into the city without anyone knowing!"

Brittany and Frankie looked confused. "You two ever think you play that game a little too much?" she asked.

"No!" said Ava and Jason together.

"*KNIGHTS OF ZEMBALORE* is amazing," Jason said. "Oh, what's your gamer name? I will add you as a friend when we finally get out of here."

"It's…" Ava said.

Jason blinked. He was sure he hadn't heard her properly. It couldn't be true. He blinked again.

"What? Say that again."

"I said my name is SparkleKitten42," grinned Ava.

"That's a pretty name," said Brittany.

"Thank you," smiled Ava. "We should team up, Jason!"

Jason felt his stomach tighten. The world blurred out of focus. SparkleKitten42. Of all the players in the game. The millions of players. *Was SHE* SparkleKitten42? The player who had been ruining his time on *KNIGHTS OF ZEMBALORE*? The player who had been ruining his *life* was *Ava*?!

"What's yours?" Ava asked.

"It doesn't matter," said Jason, looking back at the city.

"Come on; I told you mine!"

"No!" said Jason, too loudly. "Just drop it."

Ava frowned. "What's the matter with you?"

"Uh oh, something's up," mumbled Brittany.

Frankie shuffled backward a bit, trying to get off the pig.

"What's the matter?" Jason laughed bitterly. He slid off Snuffles and walked to the edge of the path. "WHAT'S THE MATTER?" he suddenly roared. "I'm *Finn2Winn*, that's what's the matter!"

Ava stared down at him from the pig.

"Oh," she said.

"Oh," he replied. "Is that all you've got to say? Oh?"

"Well-" said Ava.

"You *ruined* the game for me," said Jason. "*My* game. Your constant bullying and harassing meant that I couldn't do *anything*." He clenched his fists. "I was the top player!"

"But *everyone* wants to be top player," she said quietly.

"But it was *me*, Ava. And you ruined it!"

"I didn't think-"

"No, you didn't think," said Jason. "You never do. You just run off by yourself and don't think of anyone else."

Ava got off the pig, her eyes filled with fury and tears. She looked as if she was going to say something, but then stormed off into the woods surrounding the city.

"No, Ava, wait!" said Brittany. She rolled her eyes. "Great, Jason, you had to get all angry about your stupid game. Now we have to get her back!"

Jason felt deflated. "That wasn't - it wasn't

what I meant. I was upset…"

Brittany got down. "Well, it's too late now. Come on, Snuffles, let's go find her. Frankie, stay here."

Jason and Frankie were left alone.

"She ruined my life," Jason said, looking at Frankie. "I was right, wasn't I?"

"… …. … …. …… …"

Jason couldn't hear him, but he could almost figure out what he was saying. *Did she ruin your life or your game? They are different things.*

Frankie looked away into the distance. Jason couldn't blame him. He felt really dumb. Why had he snapped at her like that? He should have at least waited until they were out of the game.

He looked up at the sky and wondered what his dad was up to right now. Would he be worried because his son was missing? Or would he even notice that Jason wasn't locked away in his bedroom playing a game?

19. Solo Adventure

Jason blinked the tiredness out of his eyes. The world around him was dark and blurry. He had fallen asleep against a nearby tree, and when he opened his eyes fully, there was a sword pointed right at the end of his nose.

A knight dressed in silver armor with a flowing red cape, was holding the sword.

"This one's woken up," he said. "Should I stab him?"

Jason didn't hear the reply. His eyes widened with fear. He was about to beg for his life when something heavy hit him on the side of the head, and everything went black.

Wake up.

A voice. Someone Jason recognized.

Wake up, Jason. You're nearly out. Just a little more.

Ben! It was Ben's voice! Jason tried to cry out. He tried to speak, but he couldn't make a sound.

Wake up…

***

Jason opened his eyes. He was expecting a cage. A dungeon. Maybe some kind of monster. Possibly torture.

Instead, he found himself lying in a very large, comfortable bed. Sunlight streamed in through the window, lighting up a room which was twice the size of his own bedroom.

The walls and floor were made of white marble. It was decorated with flowers in golden, expensive-looking vases, large tapestries hung on every wall and a thick, red carpet on the floor.

On the ceiling were dramatic paintings of angels in clouds, standing next to kings and queens.

A large, wooden wardrobe stood at the far side of the room, and in the center, he could see a table with a steaming plate of tasty-looking food.

Next to the table, bright silver armor sparkled at him, but instead of a traditional helmet, a crown of jewels rested at the top, set into intricate metalwork.

"The crown would look good on you. I have an eye for this sort of thing."

Jason almost jumped at the voice. He could have sworn the woman now sat in a chair in the corner of the room had not been here a second before. He winced. His face felt swollen. His teeth were stinging. He tried to move, but his whole body ached.

The woman came closer.

Jason frowned.

She looked identical to Melissa, from the start of the game. The same thin body and a sharp face. But this time, she was wearing black instead of purple and she had black hair. She walked over to the armor and stroked it with a long finger, ending in a sharp, pointed nail.

"Melissa?" Jason mumbled, his tongue feeling thick in his mouth.

The woman laughed, a light and floating

laugh. "My men must have hit you harder than I thought – I'm truly sorry about that." She sat down on the side of his bed. "My name is Betrayna. You may have heard of me. Probably from my sister."

Jason's eyes widened. It hurt — a lot.

He tried to shift away on the bed, but the comforter was tucked in too tight.

"Don't worry," she said. "I'm not going to hurt you. Well, not *anymore*."

"What about my friends?" Jason asked.

She laughed again. "From the way you were treating them, I don't think you have any friends here, Jason."

Jason felt heat rising to his face. He wanted to blame the bruise, but he knew what it was. Shame.

Betrayna sat down on the bed. "Except for *me*, of course. I'll be your friend." She looked him in the eyes. Jason had not noticed before how strikingly blue they were.

"Friends," he said. It didn't sound like a bad idea at all. Jason would like to be her friend. His head felt heavy. His heartbeat thumped loudly in his ears.

"And you know what friends do?" she said. "They give each other gifts. I have a gift for you, Jason."

"A gift?"

Betrayna nodded. She smoothed out the blanket on the bed. "How would you like to be King of the World?"

Jason blinked. That sounded *great*!

"King of the World?"

"Sure!" smiled Betrayna (she had *such* a pretty smile). She stood up and walked over to the armor. "This could be yours. You could rule over everything. You could be top dog!" She held out her hand. A spade appeared there. A muddy, rusty spade. His spade. "It's better than *this*, right?

Jason's mind felt fuzzy like someone was wrapping a pillow around his brain. "But… friends."

For a moment, he could swear he saw a flash of annoyance in Betrayna's eyes. It was gone before he could say anything.

She nodded. "Okay, I see you're a tough cookie. I appreciate that." She tapped a finger against her lips. "You can have *one* friend. Which one do you want? The boy cleric? The druid?"

A smile twisted her face. "Oooooh, I know. You like the thief."

Betrayna clicked her fingers.

Pop!

Ava was suddenly standing beside the bed. She frowned, confused. Her eyes widened when she saw Jason.

"Jason! Don't li-"

Ava disappeared again.

Betrayna was suddenly next to Jason, very, *very close*.

"She can be your queen," said Betrayna. "You just need to accept my offer. Then you'll be the best of the best."

"The best of –" Words were getting very difficult.

"Number one. Just like in *KNIGHTS OF ZEMBALORE*."

Jason blinked. *KNIGHTS OF ZEMBALORE*. Jason's favorite game. He could play it for hours. Although… Now he didn't want to so much. It wasn't the same.

He didn't want to be alone anymore. If he did want to play it, it would be with someone. He might not be the best, but maybe that didn't matter.

He could play it with Ava.

Betrayna frowned. "You're doing a lot of… thinking. I don't like it. Make your choice."

CHOICE. YOU HAVE A CHOICE.

Jason looked around. He looked at the bedroom fit for a king. He looked at all the wealth and the power he could have. He looked at Betrayna, with her unnerving beauty and her bright blue eyes. Eyes like ice.

He slowly got out of bed. Betrayna smiled.

"Yes," she said. "Try on the crown. It will look good."

Jason looked up at the armor. An armor fit for a king. He turned to Betrayna.

"I choose –" He held out his hand. The spade magically appeared in it. " – my friends."

With all his might, he smashed the armor with the spade.

20. FINAL BOSS

Loading...

It wasn't like hitting metallic armor. It was like smashing glass.

The world around Jason shattered. The fancy bedroom fell away. The marble turned into dark stone. The sunlight was replaced by torches lit with cold, green fire. The whole bedroom became a long, dark hall.

Beside Jason, stood Ava, Brittany, and Frankie.

Jason turned to them. "You're okay!" he grinned.

Ava threw her arms around him. "So are you!" she said. "I'm so sorry, Jason. I wasn't thinking, you're right, I just wanted to be your friend in *KOZ* but didn't know how to ask and-"

Jason pulled her away. "No, I need to say sorry. I was a total tool. It's just a silly game. It's not real life. I'm sorry."

Ava looked up at him. "Oh, well, yeah." She grinned. "You are a tool."

Jason nodded. "Just like this spade."

"YOU'LL ALL BE SORRY," Betrayna's voice boomed around the room. A dark-robed figure with a black crown stepped out of the fire at the far end of the room. This version of Betrayna had blood-red eyes and sharp, pointed teeth. "ACTUALLY," she hissed. "YOU WON'T BE SORRY. YOU'LL BE DEAD."

She slammed her fist into the wall beside her. The whole room shook. Ava fell into Jason's arms. Brittany screamed as chunks of dark rock dislodged from the ceiling and plummeted towards her.

Frankie leaped forward, shoving his sister out of the way, holding his staff above his head. A beam of bright light burst out of the crystal and surrounded them both with a golden shield. The rocks fell around them, hitting the shield again and again. Given the look of strain on Frankie's face, he would not be able to keep them safe for long.

"FOOLISH GUARDIANS AND YOUR TRICKS. YOU WON'T BE ABLE TO – OW!" Betrayna looked down. A knife stuck out of her leg. Ava appeared out of thin air next to her.

"Um, hi?" Ava said.

Betrayna rolled her eyes and batted Ava away like she was a fly. Ava hit the wall with a sickening thump.

"No!" screamed Jason.

Jason lifted his spade above his head and charged, roaring at the top of his lungs.

Betrayna grinned and clicked her fingers.

The spade made a strange creaking sound and then shifted and twisted in Jason's hands. It wrapped around his body like a snake, and before he could stop it, he was entangled by the stretched-out metal. He couldn't move.

Betrayna stepped forward.

"I AM GOING TO ENJOY THIS," she grinned, and let out a long, cruel laugh. She pointed a finger at Jason and fire burst out in front of her. Jason closed his eyes. There was no escape.

The fire froze in mid-air.

He opened his eyes again. Everything had frozen. Ava slumped against the wall. Frankie looking down at his sister, sweating, trying to hold off the crushing stone. Brittany, hugging her brother, crying. Betrayna sneering with her final blast of fire at her fingertips. All frozen, like time itself had stopped.

"Uh..." said Jason. "Hello?"

21. Low Hit-points

"Sorry, it took a bit longer to get here than I thought it would."

Jason couldn't believe his eyes. "BEN?" he said.

Ben was standing next to Betrayna, except he looked just like Ben, not the knight version, but the Ben from before the game, who had taken the bus with Jason to Tony's Gaming Store in a black t-shirt.

He looked around, scratching his head, looking at the frozen fight. "Wow, you aren't doing great," he said. "Putting up a good fight."

"Ben?" Jason said again. "But you're, how, what?"

"It's a long story," said Ben. "Listen, you know, the company who made this game?"

"LiveReal?" said Jason.

"Yeah, my mom works for them, remember?"

Jason nodded. That was why they had gone to the game test in the first place. His mom was head of the team developing it or something.

"Well." Ben looked a bit uncomfortable. "That isn't the whole truth." He shook his head. "Let me get you out of that." Ben made a complex maneuver with his fingers. A purple circle appeared in front of him. He began to type something on it incredibly fast.

The spade wrapped around Jason disappeared.

Jason looked down: he was free. "How did you do *that*?" he asked.

"Developer's console," said Ben. "It's a special menu that lets you fiddle around with parts of the game. It's how I froze everything. It's how I skipped levels when we were about to die. It's how I stopped the exit button from working and –"

"Wait – what?" Jason walked over to Ben. "You… YOU trapped us in the game? We've been stuck here for DAYS because of YOU?!"

Ben raised his hands. "Listen, you're angry, I get it –"

"You don't get it, Ben!" Jason was shouting now. He had never been so angry. "Look at Ava! We could have died!"

Ben blinked. He stepped back. "I'm sorry. It was a stupid risk. I know that, but… but they have my mom, Jason. I haven't seen her in months! LiveReal have taken her hostage or something. I don't know. This game was the only way I could hack into their systems. But if we quit, I wouldn't have had a chance to figure it out. I HAD to do it."

"You were our friend, Ben. You could have told us," Jason said, calming down. "We would have understood."

"No," said Ben, his face hardening. "I couldn't have taken that chance. We are all guinea pigs in LiveReal's experimental program, and the only reason you are here is that I made you come here. I betrayed you. I betrayed you all."

"But Ben, we all make mistakes…"

"No," said Ben. "This wasn't a mistake. It was

a choice." He took a step forward. "Look, I'm sorry. I manipulated it all, but *I figured it out*, Jason, I know where to look next. I found out where the servers are located in the real world."

"We can find them together," said Jason.

"No, you've done enough," smiled Ben. "Listen, I've reactivated the quit command. You can leave the game at any time. You'll all leave if one of you exits." Ben stopped. He raised an eyebrow. "Wait, something's not right." There was another flurry of movement from his fingers. His eyes widened. "Oh no, oh no, oh no." He went pale. "They've figured out what I'm doing. No no no – quick!" he turned to Jason. "Quit the game! You can die in the game! You need to –"

Ben disappeared.

"BEN!" Jason cried out. He ran to where his

friend had just been standing, but there was nothing. Nothing at all.

Fire blasted into the wall next to him, sending flecks of marble everywhere.

Betrayna looked around. "HOW DID THAT MISS?" She boomed. She turned to Jason. "WHAT IS GOING ON?"

Jason dropped to his knees. Ben had disappeared again. He looked up at Betrayna.

"YOU WILL NEVER ESCAPE!" she said.

"You're wrong," Jason whispered. He tugged on his ear.

Bloop!

He pressed QUIT GAME.

The world went white.

THANK YOU FOR PLAYING!
LIVE REAL CO.
LIVE REAL.
PLAY VIRTUAL!

22. Game Credits

Jason opened his eyes. He was sitting in a chair in Tony's Gaming Store. He was back. HE WAS BACK!

Jason tugged the helmet off his head and fell forward out of his chair, gasping for breath, Fresh, real air. It was *the best*.

He looked up and around. The store was… empty? No Melissa. No scientists. No computers beeping and chirping. Just an empty store with five chairs in the middle. In them sat Ava, Brittany, Frankie and…

Ben was missing. Where was Ben?

Jason pushed himself to his feet and pulled the helmet off his friends. He put a hand on Ava's cheek. She was warm. "Ava," he gasped. "Ava, are you okay?"

Stunning brown eyes met his. She smiled. "Jason?" she said.

Jason was shoved to the side as Brittany grabbed him and hugged him. "We're free! We did it!" She turned towards Frankie, scooping him up off the chair and hugging him tightly. "You saved me! WE'RE FREE!" Brittany paused. "I need to update my Instagram – my followers are NOT GOING TO BELIEVE THIS!" She pulled her phone out of her pocket and kissed the screen.

Frankie rolled his eyes, but he was smiling.

Ava frowned. "Where is everyone?" she asked. "Where is Ben?" She looked at Jason. "What happened? How did we get out of the game?

Jason looked at her. He thought about telling them everything, about Ben's betrayal, about LiveReal's experiment. "No idea," he lied. "What should we do now?"

Brittany looked at her phone. She frowned too. "That can't be right," she said.

"What?" said Ava.

"It's only been… twenty minutes since we sat down in the chairs. "

"But we were in there for DAYS!" said Jason. "How is that possible?"

"I'm sure Ben would know," Ava mumbled.

The shop seemed bigger and emptier than ever before.

"I guess we should go home," said Jason.

***

Ava and Jason sat next to each other on the bus and didn't speak. Ava looked at her phone – more missed calls and messages. She put her phone away as Jason stood up to get off.

"Jason," she said.

"Yeah?" said Jason.

Ava bit her lip. She wanted to say something, about what had happened, about how she felt, but all she managed to get out was: "I'll see you around?"

"Yeah," smiled Jason. "I'll add you as a friend on *KOZ*."

Ava nodded.

He left the bus.

As she watched the bus pull away, she kicked herself. Why couldn't she just say what she wanted?

***

Jason sat on his bed, wiping a smear of spaghetti sauce from his cheek. He turned on his games console out of habit. The menu of *KNIGHTS OF ZEMBALORE* opened on his screen.

He stared at it, sighed, and flopped back onto his bed. The *last* thing he wanted to do was play a game.

At least everything was back to normal.

Boring, everyday normal.

Bla-bling!

Jason frowned at his phone that lay on the bed next to him.

He picked it up. Who was messaging him at this time?

It was a message, but the phone said it came from 5JuI"s!sshf#@?.

"What?" he said, sitting up. He opened the message.

It simply read:

Ear.

What was that supposed to mean? It was probably just some kind of problem with his phone.

He was lying back down on his bed when a cold realization dawned on him.

"No," he said, sitting back up. "It can't be. It's impossible." He reached up to his ear, his hand freezing in place. "Please, no," he said. "Please. Please."

He tugged on his ear.
BLOOP!
A menu popped open in front of him.
His eyes widened in fear.
THEY WERE STILL IN THE GAME.

Thank you for reading TRAPPED
Book 1 *The Virtual Guardians*

If you enjoyed this book, could you please
leave a review?
Thank you
Katrina and Richard

Book 2 – Home Sweet Home

Some other books you may enjoy…

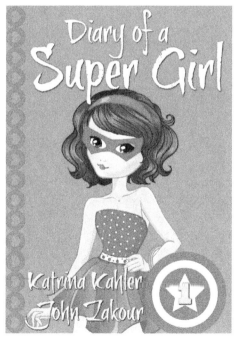

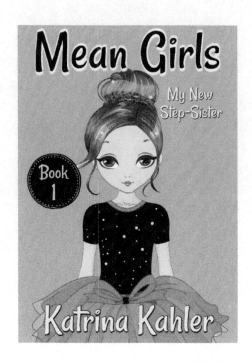

We really appreciate and love
our readers! You are amazing!

You can subscribe to our website
www.bestsellingbooksforkids.com
so we can notify you as soon as
we release a new book.

Please 👍 Katrina's Facebook page
https://www.facebook.com/katrinaauthor
and follow Katrina on Instagram
@katrinakahler

Printed in Great Britain
by Amazon